YOUR LIFE IS FORFEIT

YOUR LIFE IS FORFEIT

JUDGE, JURY, & EXECUTIONER™ BOOK FOUR

CRAIG MARTELLE

MICHAEL ANDERLE

Craig Martelle Social

Website & Newsletter:
http://www.craigmartelle.com

Facebook:
https://www.facebook.com/AuthorCraigMartelle/

Michael Anderle Social

Website: http://kurtherianbooks.com/

Email List: http://kurtherianbooks.com/email-list/
Facebook:
https://www.
facebook.com/TheKurtherianGambitBooks/

THE YOUR LIFE IS FORFEIT TEAM

Thanks to our Beta Readers

Micky Cocker
James Caplan
Kelly O'Donnell

Thanks to the JIT Readers

Mary Morris
Keith Verret
John Ashmore
Kelly O'Donnell
Daniel Weigert
James Caplan
Larry Omans
Paul Westman
Peter Manis
Micky Cocker

If I've missed anyone, please let me know!

Editor
Lynne Stiegler

We can't write without those who support us
On the home front, we thank you for being there for us

We wouldn't be able to do this for a living if it weren't for our
readers
We thank you for reading our books

"Look who the cat dragged in!" Red laughed as he finished another set using the bench press, turning the massive pile of weight over to Lindy. "What happened to your hair?"

"Don't listen to him. Stretch, and let's get you started," Rivka told Jay, who was participating in her first post-Pod-doc visit to the gym.

Jay motioned for the Magistrate to join her in the corner for a private conversation. The two women huddled together, and Jay looked over her shoulder before whispering, "He's right. After the treatment, my hair's curly and I can't do anything with it."

Rivka shrugged. "My eyes weren't always this color. The Pod-doc changes us."

"But..." Jay protested. She pulled the collar of her shirt down to reveal a single black hair the length of her hand growing out of the middle of her chest. She wrapped it around a finger and yanked it out, tossing it aside. Almost instantly it reappeared, and within seconds it had grown back to its previous length. "I don't like that, and I don't feel right. I don't feel stronger or more invincible or anything like you guys seem to."

"After our workout, we'll get some answers. Maybe your nanocytes need to settle in. Give them a vigorous shake-up, and you may be amazed."

"What about this?" Jay pointed at the hair dangling from her shirt.

"I don't know what to tell you about that. I can't tell you it's not weird."

"I don't want it."

"There are a lot of things in life that we don't want but get to cope with anyway. Maybe the nanos determined you needed it for some reason. Tiny alien rappelling lessons?"

Jay rolled her eyes as Rivka clapped her on the shoulder.

"Come on, we've got a lot of reps to do before we can call it a day."

Lindy grunted with effort as she tried to keep up with Red. He beamed with pride after each completed rep and glanced at the stack repeatedly. "A new record!" he declared when Lindy finished and the plates thumped into the rack.

She stood and stretched. "Felt good, but that's it. Unless I get my skeleton upgraded to titanium, I'm not sure my body can handle any more. I can feel my bones straining. How screwed up is that?"

Red laughed softly before giving her a sweaty hug. "I feel it, too. Maybe we've hit the limit of enhanced human endurance. Look at that stack!" The modified weight rack registered upward of a metric ton, and they were lifting all of it. "We don't know until we go beyond."

Rivka pushed Red aside and straddled the bench. She put her feet up and pushed the stack upward, easing it back into place after five reps. "I see what you mean." She cut the weight to a single plate—a mere two hundred pounds—and pointed for Jay to take her place.

The young woman with the curly black hair looked skeptical as she laid back, braced herself and strained against the bar. The muscles in her arms bulged and tightened, but the stack didn't move.

"That's weird. She should be able to push that on her worst day," Red remarked, pursing his lips and watching intently as he tried to figure out what was wrong. Lindy crossed her arms and clicked her tongue.

"Enough weights," Rivka directed, not wanting Jay to be embarrassed or further skylined as incapable. The young woman looked worried as Rivka pulled her upright. "Time for some gentle sparring."

She looked slyly at Red. The two contenders always ended up in the ring last. Rivka was smaller, but a heavyweight in ability. She trained hard with Grainger every chance she got. Being a Magistrate was dangerous enough without going at it half-assed.

"I'll get to you," she told him. "Come on, Jay. Let's work on some counter-moves. Try to punch me in the head."

Rivka raised her hands and bobbed lightly on the balls of her feet. The impact came before anyone saw the movement. Rivka's head snapped back, and she found herself falling. She landed flat on her back and Jay rushed forward to kneel beside her, worry creasing her brow. "I'm sorry! I don't know what happened."

Red reached down and yanked Rivka to her feet. "Did you see that?" he asked.

"I saw nothing," Rivka mumbled. "How'd you do that?"

"Maybe we should try the bag?" Lindy suggested, hoping to avoid being Jay's next victim.

Jayita sat on the mat and hugged her knees. "I'm so sorry," she stammered.

"For what?" Rivka asked. Jay mumbled unintelligibly.

Ankh? We could use your expertise in the Magistrate's gym. Jay's nanocytes are doing weird things, Rivka requested, using their internal comm system.

Interesting. I worked on the programming because we can't have her all bulky like the rest of you. I'll be right there, the Crenellian replied.

Rivka shook her head at the reply. "Ankh is coming. He said we're bulky, and he couldn't allow Jay to be like us, whatever that means. In the meantime, how about we do a little speed check?"

"I like being bulky." Red flexed a massive bicep.

"I'm not sure I like being called bulky, but there are advantages in our line of work." Lindy smiled at Red.

"*Our* line of work," Red emphasized, swelling with joy at having found his soulmate. He gave her a quick peck on the cheek.

"My big, bad bodyguard," Rivka cooed, flexing her bicep. "Am *I* bulky?"

Red looked away, and Lindy shrugged.

"You have been saved from our fate, it appears. Come and take a shot at the bag. I think you're going to find a skill that none of us have."

Jay reluctantly stood and faced off against the bag. She slapped it a few times.

"Not like that!" Rivka stood behind the bag, took hold, and braced herself. "Hit it like you're fighting for your life. Practice how you play, as the saying goes."

Jay bounced on her feet and punched—wildly, but blindingly fast. The only sign that she'd swung was the sound of her hand hitting the bag. Dents appeared where she'd struck. With each impact, Rivka grunted from the shock.

"Try to kick it," Red suggested.

Jay bent at the waist as she executed a side-kick, sending Rivka off her feet to land in a heap. The bag swung freely as the Magistrate laid on the floor. Jay hopped and kicked it again. No one saw her foot as the bag careened off the ceiling. She tried to catch it when it flew back toward her, hitting Jay in the chest and knocking her to the floor opposite Rivka.

"Let me see if I understand this. You can strike at light speed but get knocked over by a feather?"

"We'll work on that," Ankh said.

"How long have you been standing there?" Red asked, surprised that the Crenellian had snuck up on him.

"Does that matter?" Ankh asked, looking up with his usual blank stare. Red shook his head and was first to look away. "I've programmed the nanos for maximum speed at the cost of strength. Jay will not have your density; her muscles are optimized for something more in line with her personality. Speed will save her life, not strength."

"I would like to think that her mind will save her life rather than any physical enhancements," Rivka offered.

"I'd like to think that you won't put me in harm's way." Jay stood as tall as she was able, towering over the Crenellian but shorter than the other three. "Or Ankh."

Red and Lindy waited for Rivka to answer. "Or that," she muttered with little confidence.

Jay started to laugh. "So, I'm okay?"

"You are more than okay, Jayita," Ankh stated. "You are faster than what they used to call vampiric speed. You will also be able to take a bullet without dying, although it'll be painful and take a long time to heal. When your adrenaline pumps, you should be able to see a bullet in flight and step out of its way. You won't be able to dodge a laser or most energy beams, unfortunately."

"She'll only be able to dodge some of the energy beams, but all bullets? Where has this been all my life?" Red wondered.

Ankh stared at the big man. Red found himself looking away yet again. Lindy caught his chin and pulled his face toward hers.

He smiled and shrugged. "He can probably kill us with his brain, so let's not push it."

Tod Mackestray was a Blokite. His squarish head topped his broad shoulders, giving the impression of a blockhouse on top of a small mountain. As wide as he was tall, he moved in a graceless waddle. Keen eyes on the front and sides of his head missed nothing and helped his focused mind assimilate information. That was critical in running his budding empire.

The only thing Tod sold was influence, from blackmail, threats, and protection rackets to simple leverage. The Blokite moved people into key positions and just as quickly moved them out. He thought of it like chess.

His bodyguards knew it was a dangerous business. At least once a week, the leveraged would try to strike back, but they were amateurs in the ways of the universe. He had yet to break into the highest ranks of power, but that time was coming.

And soon.

Mackestray's lip curled when he thought about it. Upcoming elections. There was nothing democratic about it. The votes had been logged into the system before the first voter cast her ballot. The process didn't matter since the outcome depended on the final tally. His boy would win by a sound one percent.

It was worth a cool million credits, which was still a steep discount based on influence from the back end. In Tod's mind, having a hotline to the chairman's ear was worth more than credits. The world would be shaped under his influence. And if the chairman tried to cut ties? The Blokite had the evidence of vote tampering that he'd share with the public.

It was called leverage, and Tod Mackestray used it like a surgeon used a scalpel.

Grainger sat in a dark corner where he could see out the vast All Guns Blazing window while also seeing the entrance, his double Flaming Buki Hole forgotten on the table before him.

The datapad next to the drink buzzed, drawing his eye. High Chancellor Wyatt. He looked around to make sure no one was nearby, tipped the screen, and tapped to answer. "What can I do for you, High Chancellor?"

"We have a couple big cases on the docket, and I don't see that any Magistrates have been assigned." The older man smiled, but his voice was cold.

"Not all cases," Grainger replied. He tapped through his screens while the reduced image of the High Chancellor stared at him from the upper left corner. Two Magistrates were already on their way. He tapped a couple of buttons. "Jael and Chi are looking into the gang violence in the Tricott Cluster, and Buster is already digging into the government corruption case. I put two on one case, High Chancellor, based on what we learned working as a team. Sometimes it takes two sets of eyes to get the law and the case right. That one could be dangerous."

Wyatt looked disappointed but answered pleasantly, "That fills two, but we still have a couple major issues out there, and we're slowly building a backlog. What are you going to assign to Rivka?"

"She's asked for some time off to take care of a personal matter."

The High Chancellor sat up straight and leaned toward the screen. "What kind of personal matter?"

"She wouldn't tell me, but I think she's going after Red's former employers—the ones who put a price on his head," Grainger whispered at the screen.

Wyatt clicked his tongue and nodded slowly. "Then she

is going to do legal work that needs to be done. Give her all the support she needs but won't ask for, and log it as an official case sanctioned by me, classified to the highest degree. Our eyes only."

"I'll inform her at once," Grainger said, but Wyatt shook his head.

"She shouldn't keep secrets from us, so we'll keep this under our hats, so to speak. She's going to a dangerous place. I'll inform the Bad Company that we may need their services."

"Nothing like a mechanized combat unit and destroyer to emphasize certain legal interpretations." Grainger checked over his shoulder. He was alone. "I'll leave her to it. The Magistrate ships have trackers, so we'll know where *Peacekeeper* is at all times."

"Is that the name she gave it? Maybe she needs a bigger ship. She has a way of rescuing the distraught and building followers."

Grainger laughed easily. "She does indeed. I think the only thing keeping her from taking on more is the size of her ship. I think the corvette might be best."

Wyatt delivered a genuine smile. "Keep me informed." The older man's face faded from the screen. Grainger shut down his pad, shoved it inside his jacket, and stood, promptly bumping into someone. Rivka looked up at him.

"Who you talking with?"

Grainger stepped back smoothly to stay out of Rivka's reach. "When are you headed out?" he countered.

"After you give me some answers." Rivka slowly extended her hand. Grainger picked up a plate and used it as a shield to fend her off.

"We all need our secrets, don't you think? Maybe you tell me straight up: where are *you* going?"

Rivka stuffed her hand into her pocket. "You are correct, Grainger, but don't let it go to your head. I'm sure you'll be wrong next time. We find ourselves at an impasse, so with that, I'll return to my ship. I have some prep work to do for my *time off*."

"We got your back. Just let us know, and we'll be there," Grainger told her.

"I know. I'm not quite ready to share yet, but when I am, you'll be the first."

Grainger leaned against the table as Rivka maneuvered her way through the bar and out the front, nodding and waving at the staff as she went. He looked at his unfinished drink, put his plate back on the table, and tried to remember where he had been going. When nothing came to mind, he returned to his drink, finished it, and called for another.

He turned his datapad on and started reading an old-time science fiction novel.

CHAPTER TWO

Rivka scowled at the screen while reclining in the captain's chair. "You haven't found a damn thing? How is that possible?"

"Mister Tod Mackestray maintains a non-presence. He doesn't exist, as far as the Federation is concerned," Chaz, the ship's artificial intelligence, replied.

"He has to exist, or at least his companies do. You know the old adage, Chaz. Follow the money. You've been given access to how Red was paid back then. What did you find?"

"The company that paid him had exactly one employee. As soon as Red left, that company dissolved. There are too many companies with only one employee. I cannot canvass them all."

"Ankh is on board. Did you ask Erasmus and him for help?" Ankh's custom-designed AI called Erasmus had been instrumental in helping resolve Rivka's previous two cases. Erasmus lived inside the Crenellian's head.

"Ankh is not currently on board. He left shortly after Jayita departed for work."

"We're going to need their help. Hang on." Rivka opened the hatch on the bridge and yelled, "Red! Get your ass in here."

She laughed softly as she waited.

"Really? This is how we talk to each other now?" Red asked. Lindy was at his side dressed in shorts and one of Red's old t-shirts.

"It isn't. I'm sorry, big man. I wanted to tell you that Chaz is unable to find any data on your old boss."

"Which one?"

"Mackestray," Chaz clarified.

"That guy was a total snake, for a Blokite anyway. He jumped from planet to planet, never setting up in one place for too long. I don't know any way to track him. He didn't share any particulars of his businesses, but he bought and sold influence."

"How could a ghost sell influence?"

"That's probably the *best* way to sell it. He keeps his hands clean while threatening to blackmail others. Pay to keep him quiet or pay to dethrone an opponent. Politics is a nasty business, and thus a fertile place for scum like Mackestray. Before you say it, I thought he was a politician aspiring for some high office because of the people he was meeting with until I heard the conversations, and then I couldn't get out of there fast enough."

"Who is the other guy, and how'd you come to work for him?" Rivka asked.

"The other is an interesting character. His name is K'Twillis, an Aborginian. He's half-plant, half-humanoid, and needs a certain amount of solar radiation each day for photosynthesis. It's a strange race. He speaks by way of a microphone thing that he carries and surrounds himself with a security team of locals and aliens."

"Since the Federation is race-neutral, we can't track aliens based on their species, but we *can* search for them based on their dietary restrictions if they've registered them with the authorities," Chaz remarked. "A quick search does not find an individual named K'Twillis anywhere in the Federation."

"Of course not. You left his service why?" Rivka asked.

"Mining. He runs operations that rip gashes in planets' surfaces," Red replied.

Rivka chewed on her lip. "You don't strike me as an eco-warrior, and modern reclamation technologies can clean things like that up in short order, so why did that bother you?"

"It cuts me deeply that you wouldn't think I care about the environment." Red winked at the Magistrate. "It's not that it can't be reclaimed, but his methods were to forcibly displace the locals, or kill them if they didn't move. Have you ever gone into someone's home in the middle of the night and torn them from their beds? I have. One time. I wouldn't do it after that. The people were terrified and for good reason. K'Twillis sent crews in and strip-mined a place, abandoning it after he got what he wanted."

"Mining operations have huge footprints. Illegal mining? How in the hell does he get away with that?"

"Buys off local officials."

"But then it would be legal mining, based on the corruption of the locals. Bribery isn't a big crime. Selling out your planet? Those people need to be on the receiving end of some Magistrate Justice."

"That, too," Red admitted. "But we leaned on them as necessary."

"Chaz, can you track strip mining operations from..."

"Try Remus Six," Red offered.

"From Remus Six. Let's see if he's leaving a trail across the galaxy."

"This would be easier if Erasmus could help," Chaz requested.

Ankh. Could you and Erasmus return to Peacekeeper, please? We need your help, Rivka sent using their internal comm. She expected an answer right away but didn't get one.

"Chaz, will you locate Ankh, please?" Worry lines creased Rivka's brow.

"He's in the Pod-doc on Level Four."

"I'll be back," Rivka said, running for the hatch. Red fell in behind her, and Lindy behind him. The Magistrate didn't question it. She accepted that they would join her and hoped she didn't need their expertise.

Jay leaned against the wall while the technician kept his hands off the controls. His arm twitched because he wanted to make adjustments, but a tsk from Jay stopped him. Ankh and Erasmus were in control, even from inside the Pod-doc.

When the cycle ended, the door opened, and Ankh climbed out and got adressed. Jay kneeled to be at eye-level with him. "You don't look any different."

"I wouldn't suppose so, no," the Crenellian replied evenly. He didn't bother to thank the technician. That wasn't his way. He walked out without a further word, stopping when Rivka nearly ran into him.

"Ankh! I was worried about you," the Magistrate admitted. Red and Lindy visually scoured the corridor to ensure that Rivka was safe before they turned their attention to the small alien.

"Why?" Ankh asked innocently.

"I didn't know you were going to..." Her voice trailed off as she looked him up one side and down the other. "What did you have done?"

"The actions on Collum Gate convinced me that I needed to survive getting shot, so I've programmed my nanocytes to respond to injuries, plus I enhanced my skeleton, including my cranium. It is protected by a titanium alloy now. Can't risk Erasmus."

"Or yourself," Jay suggested with a smile.

Rivka stood with her hands on her hips, unsure of how she was feeling. "I don't know if I'm supposed to be angry that you didn't tell me or happy that you are now better protected. And why aren't you at work?" Rivka raised an eyebrow at Jayita.

"I got fired."

"I have been around humans long enough to know that your emotions are your undoing," Ankh started. "I do what needs to be done. I am on the team for that purpose. Do you trust me?"

Rivka stammered before replying. "I'm sorry, Ankh. You are correct."

"Of course I am." Ankh's expression never changed. He wore his night-vision goggles on his forehead.

Rivka wanted to call him an ass but thought better of it.

She needed him more than he needed her, and he wasn't trying to be abrasive. Ankh was hopelessly honest. Ankh was Ankh.

"We need your help, Ankh. We're looking for a couple of individuals who don't want to be found."

Ankh looked up at her. "Is it a case or a mission?"

Rivka smiled. "We'll call it a reckoning, but we'll stay within the framework of the law. We have to."

"Yes, yes. Let's get back to the ship, and you can tell me all about it." Ankh strolled off at his slow pace, but Red picked him up. The bodyguard's patience was extremely limited, and Ankh didn't mind getting a ride.

"You said you were fired," Rivka started. "Why?"

"They said they didn't want my kind in there."

"What did they mean by that?" Rivka questioned.

"Someone working there for the perks, or not a member of the family, or hair too blue, or whatever."

Rivka's lip twitched, and she growled deep in her throat. "Detour."

"I thought we might," Red remarked. Lindy nodded, taking the lead to hurry the group toward the spa.

"What are you going to do?" Jay asked.

"What I always do: learn the truth."

Jay hung her head and followed. Rivka wondered if Jay had been completely honest, but didn't press her and avoided touching her. The Magistrate knew that Jay was upset, but couldn't pinpoint why. She'd find out soon enough.

K'Twillis shambled through the park, spreading his leafy arms to catch as much sunshine as possible. Two bodyguards walked nearby, hands conspicuously clutching automatic weapons. In a place like Capstan, weapons were rarely allowed. Those with them were given a wide berth, which was exactly how K'Twillis liked it.

He removed a comm device from the foliage surrounding his body and held it up to what passed for a mouth. "Do we have the permits yet?" he asked in the whistling and rustling that passed for the Aborginian language. The device converted it to Galactic Standard.

"Not yet. They seem to think that operations are already underway. They want to visit the site to understand the boundaries."

"We've been working for two weeks now. Under no circumstances are they to visit the site. Show them the video."

"I did, and they aren't convinced. They want to see it," the voice on the other end said, his pitch increasing with each word.

K'Twillis clicked off and called a new contact. "He's finished his usefulness. Replace him with someone who will do as I ask."

"It'll be done today," the other voice replied, and the link was cut.

"What do you think?" the Aborginian asked no one in particular. "Beautiful days should have beautiful deeds by which to remember them."

The bodyguards maintained their distance and their vigils.

The old woman at the desk crossed her arms and scowled at the unseemly group that stormed into the spa's foyer. "You are banned. You no come back!" the woman declared, shaking a finger at Jay as she peeked out from behind Red's bulk.

"Why is she banned?" Rivka demanded, moving close. The woman stood her ground. Rivka smiled pleasantly and touched the woman on the arm. "I asked why she was banned."

"She was a bad employee. She don't take reservations!"

Rivka saw gaps in the schedule where there could have been massage appointments.

"Jay?" She turned a cold glare toward the young woman with the tight curls.

"They were waffling about their appointments. I couldn't convince them to reserve a spot." Jay lifted her head and stared back at the old woman. "She raised the prices, and is blaming me that people think it's too expensive."

Rivka rolled her eyes, sorry that she'd put herself in the middle of it. The old woman's guilt rose to the surface before quickly subsiding.

"We're out of here," Rivka said and twirled a finger in the air to indicate that they were leaving. Ankh's eyes were unfocused. Rivka wondered what he was doing but wouldn't ask. Some things were better left unknown.

"You go!" the old woman repeated.

Rivka stopped and shook her head. She turned back

until she was nose to nose with the woman. "If you want me to shut this place down, say one more word."

The proprietor looked like she was going to say something, but stopped, re-crossed her arms and glared at the group. Rivka hurried away so she didn't have to make good on her threat.

"Jay," Rivka said calmly. "Would you come a little closer, please?"

The young woman was reluctant but worked her way to Rivka's side. "Are you going to punish me?"

"No. I think you're doing enough of that yourself, but listen to me. You are never to go back there. Maybe you're not a salesman, but you can't keep slots empty just so you can get a deep discount on a massage. That's not cool."

"I know, but they were all angry at the new prices and I couldn't fill the schedule. I can only apologize so much. I took the slots so they didn't lose too much money."

"I understand," Rivka said, stopping to hug the young woman. "It looked like a good fit, but it wasn't. You *have* a job, so let's get you better suited for it. I'd like you and Lindy to go to the gym for a workout. Red, Ankh, and I have a few things we need to do to prepare for our next case, so we'll be returning to the ship."

"I don't feel like working out," Jay muttered.

"That's your job, and you need to go do it. We don't get to pick our moods in our line of work. Consider this good practice. We'll meet you at the ship when you're finished."

CHAPTER THREE

Tod Mackestray lounged in an antechamber of the governor's palace, the nicest home on Amberstrom. Located in the Gridlow Expanse, the series of six habitable planets had banded together to join the Federation. They operated under one umbrella, which created more travel than Tod wanted.

He grumbled, "Every time I leave one place for another, the natives run wild and I have to waste time getting them back under control." He sneered at the thought. "What to do about that? I need to leave an agent behind, but I don't trust anyone enough to let them operate in my name."

He paced in his rented office paid for by a fake shell company. He never left a footprint of his passing—not on the tile floor, and not in the business world. Alone with his thoughts, he often talked to himself because he considered that he gave himself the best advice. He trusted no one else with the insight of his business.

Which is what he told the politicians. "It's not personal. It's only business."

For the price they paid, they were either shielded from public scrutiny or their opponents subjected to it. It was the most personal of things, one's reputation. But it was about Mackestray making money. If both sides tried to pay, the higher bidder would emerge unscathed.

He sat at the massive desk that had come with the office. No one in their right mind would attempt to move such a thing. He leaned back and kicked his feet up onto the desk, and the chair groaned under his weight. Blokites were top-heavy, evolved like musk oxen to withstand blows to the head and shoulders.

"Margaret, please connect me with the chairman."

"Of course," the AI responded over the desk comm's speaker.

"Chairman Tip Nel's office," a young woman's voice answered.

"I'm sorry. This was supposed to be the chairman's direct line," Tod blurted.

"There is no direct line to the chairman. All calls are routed through this office. May I help you?"

"Yes. Connect me to Chairman Nel."

"May I tell him who's calling?"

"Mackestray," Tod said. He needed his name to strike fear into the hearts of any who heard it. There were footprints that he wouldn't leave, and there were hurricanes that appeared from nowhere, carving a wide swath across the land and disappearing just as quickly.

A gruff voice answered, "Mister Mackestray. The chairman would like to meet with you to personally thank you for your assistance in the last election. Would you be available later today?"

Tod clenched his fists and ground his teeth. When he relaxed enough, he reached a finger to the comm system and tapped it off. His AI had routed the signal off planet to make it untraceable. He would use that same anonymity for his next step.

"Margaret. Please connect me with Fil Pol."

"Of course," the ever-pleasant AI replied.

"Pol," the woman's voice answered.

"You know that you won the election, right?" Tod started.

"Who is this?" she asked.

"I'm the one who fixed the election for Tip Nel. Look at your screen. Here is a sample of the evidence I have of his crime. What is it worth to you to have this election overturned and yourself installed once the real numbers come to light?"

There was a long delay. Margaret showed the politician on screen, her camera tapped without her knowledge. Her brow furrowed in thought as a wide range of emotions crossed her face.

"I think you should simply come clean, for the good of the people," she finally suggested.

"Anytime a politician opens their mouth, bullshit spews." Tod snorted. "My price is a half a million credits. He paid me a million, but I'm willing to give you a cut rate because he's reneged on our deal."

"How do you know I won't do the same thing?" Her head hung down, and she spoke with a quiver in her voice.

"Because once you get in bed with me, there is no getting out or you will be destroyed, as I'm going to destroy Chairman Nel. I will help you get the office. That's my business. If you want to be an honest politician while you're there, that's your business. I don't care about that, although I may need a favor every now and then. Half a mil is the cheapest I have ever sold a planet's leadership, so you will still owe me. Do you think you can take care of these people better than Nel?"

She nodded, but Tod waited until she spoke.

"I don't have half a million," she admitted.

"You will once you are in office. I sign contracts based on people's word. Do you give your word?"

She leaned forward and hung her head before standing, then laced her fingers behind her back as she stood tall, acting as if she were speaking to an adoring crowd. "I am the right person to be the Chairman of Regola Seven. This planet needs strong leadership to escape the yoke of our neighbors and become self-sufficient. I have a plan. Yes, whoever you are. I agree to your terms. What is your time-line for implementation?"

"Mackestray is the name. The newsfeeds will be flooded within minutes. Core data will go to every prosecutor's office on the planet. The data and allegations will also be sent for review by Federation jurisprudence. Make no mistake. Tip Nel will not be the chairman come tomorrow."

"Mister Mackestray. I can't say that it's been a pleasure, or that I'm comfortable paying half a million credits to confirm an election that I won fairly." She started shaking her head.

"In politics, it's not who earned the most votes that matters. It's who counts those votes. Please find my payment information on your screen. Write it down since the information will disappear as soon as I cancel this connection. There will be no digital record of our conversation or that I even exist. Please abide by our agreement. Don't make me destroy you, too."

As soon as she had written down the information from the screen, he clicked off.

"Margaret, please execute program Nuclear Depth Bomb Tip Nel."

"Executing," the AI confirmed.

You got that right, Tod thought. *How* dare *you fuck with me? I have your million, and now I have an example of what happens if you try to turn on me. You'll be eating out of a garbage can inside a week.*

"Margaret, It's time for us to leave. Have a cab pick me up outside for the trip to the spaceport. I'll retire to orbit and watch from there." Tod took a handkerchief from his pocket and wiped the top of the desk. "This still doesn't solve the problem of how to maintain an effective presence when I'm not here." He wiped the door handle on his way out. "It'll come to me."

He started to whistle as he headed for the elevator, handkerchief in hand to wipe down everything else on his way from the building.

"Erasmus, please show Chaz how it's done," Ankh requested for everyone's edification. He didn't need to speak aloud and rarely did; only when he was trying to make a point with the lesser beings.

Rivka rolled her eyes and willed her patience to keep

her from arguing. Red rolled out the bench and dialed the magnetic bar to a challenging resistance before lying back and pounding out a set.

"I'll be on the bridge," the Magistrate said over her shoulder, stating the obvious as her weak jab at Ankh. The hatch closed behind her. She stopped at the sight of the grey furball curled in the middle of the captain's chair. "Hamlet, you need to get a life," she told the cat.

She picked him up, earning herself a scratched arm before settling into the chair with him on her lap. The cat never opened his eyes. She watched the cut on her arm close, always fascinated by how the nanocytes responded to her injuries, while casually stroking the cat's soft fur.

"Chaz, don't take offense at Erasmus or Ankh." She wasn't sure who she was trying to soothe with her words.

"I do not. Erasmus is much smarter than I. He has already created a worm tracker to pull the disparate elements that might fit the profile of either of the parties Vered named. I have high hopes that we will be on our way shortly."

"I like your positivity, Chaz. While we're waiting, connect me to Grainger, please."

The screen shifted, and Grainger's face appeared. "Hey! Why are you on my pad?"

"I'm calling you."

"You're calling me what?" he countered before shaking his head and continuing, "This could be the first time you've ever called me during the day. I feel I should be honored, but that also makes this strange. Should I be worried?"

"We're going after Red's former employers. I can't allow

the price to remain on his head. After what we went through on Collum Gate, we can't have random people shooting at us. We get enough of that because of me."

"Tell me something I don't know." Grainger smiled and wiggled his fingers at the screen. "These guys are criminals, right?"

"As far as I know. I trust Red, and he says they break the law as part of their business."

"Then it's a Federation matter. Don't forget the part where they put a hit on him. That makes it our business, so for the record, it's an official investigation."

"So I don't have to take vacation time, and I'll get my normal pay? You're the best, Leibowitz."

"Leibchein. It's *Leibchein*."

"I just wanted to hear you say it. My day is now complete." Rivka drew a finger across her throat, and Chaz cut the signal. "Either Grainger is getting slower, or my game has dramatically improved. What do you think, Chaz?"

"I think you have game."

"I got game!" Rivka declared. The cat stretched, exposing his needle-like claws. She stopped moving, and he relaxed into her lap.

Erasmus spoke through the bridge's speakers. "I believe we should start on Remus Six and follow K'Twillis' path from there."

"I said that two days ago." Rivka stared at the screen as a star map slowly took shape. At the bottom left was Remus Six. A myriad of systems filled the rest of the screen. Some of them started to flash.

"What you see flashing are the potential sites that

K'Twillis moved to following his operation on Remus. He may have gone to all of them, but there is some overlap on timing. If there is only one of him, one of these is a false trail. The other is not, and that is where we'll pick up the trail. I suggest we visit each planet in order to build a more complete profile. With your talent, we will be able to glean more information from the officials that he 'influenced.'"

"Influenced. Coerced. Strong-armed. Blackmailed. Killed. I think a number of terms could apply. K'Twillis is a shambling Aborginian. He should stand out anywhere except a jungle planet with sentient flora," Rivka commented. "And what about Tod Mackestray?"

"Mister Mackestray's profile is much more difficult to build. Of nine-hundred and forty-seven elections, corruption or illegal influence was claimed in nearly nine hundred of them."

"No politician, no matter what the race, believes that they can lose a fair election. It's the nature of the business. I just want to find him. I don't care about influence-peddling among politicians. Are any of them starting wars?"

"No more than usual."

"Define 'usual,' Erasmus."

"One percent. We have nine of them beating war drums, so to speak."

"We'll avoid those nine areas. Wait, put them on screen."

Lights started to flash, creating an arrow that pointed at Remus Six.

"I'm not sure that falls into our definition of the word 'usual.'"

"I appreciate your human insight. The geographic view

suggests that these are not random. However, when I rotate this three-dimensionally, the apparent line becomes more random."

"Show the Gates between those systems."

"From any one of those systems to any of the others takes at least two Gate transits. In most cases, it's three, and for the two systems farthest out, it's four."

"Back to random chance, then. Don't rule out that our boy isn't the one starting these wars. How would he profit from a planet going to war if he only sold influence?"

The hatch slid open, and Red walked in. "He charges them to end the war."

"From what you knew of him, was he the type to get off on starting wars?"

"He seemed like he wanted the people he put in power to *stay* in power. He saw that as doubling his influence because he could call in favors. You see, blackmailers never stop asking to be paid, even if it's not in credits. The well never runs dry. The Mackestrays of the universe will suck every bit of life from their victims and then demand one more drop of blood."

"I thought these people were his clients?" Rivka rubbed her chin in thought.

"They are all victims, although some pay more for the pleasure. The best thing to do if you're on the wrong end of Tod Mackestray is disappear."

"Public service positions, yet these people want them badly enough to pay a fortune to help them cheat. And then their roles are so fragile, they're willing to pay anything to keep them. I can't wrap my head around the logic because it makes no sense to me."

"That's why Tod Mackestray exists. It makes perfect sense to him. He understands who his potential clients are, and where their weak spots are. He sticks a pry bar in and starts leaning on it. In the end, they all come around."

"Are you getting this, Erasmus and Chaz? Can you make heads or tails of this information to better refine your search?" Rivka asked.

"Yes. This has been most informative. With the latest information, I am positive that we need to go to Remus Six as soon as possible. Chaz will make preparations to leave."

"Belay that," Rivka announced. "Lindy and Jay aren't on board yet. We'll leave as soon as they've returned."

"Recall them at once!" Erasmus demanded.

Rivka tilted her head and looked at the screen. "Is that you, Ankh? It sure sounds like you. And no. They will finish their workout." Rivka looked over her shoulder. "It's been…what, eight months since you were on Remus Six?"

"Right around that," Red confirmed.

Lindy and Jay, please return to the Peacekeeper *as soon as possible. We need to get going. Erasmus thinks he has a lead.*

Lindy was flat on her back. Nanocytes rushed to her broken jaw and split lips. Blood streamed from both nostrils and down the sides of her face, and her eyes started to glaze over from shock.

"I am so sorry!" Jay cried, kneeling next to her friend to help her sit up.

Lindy blinked while her head lolled and moaned from the pain of her broken face, then coughed and turned to spit blood. When the blood stopped flowing from her nose, she faced Jay. "Did I at least hurt your hand with my face?" She chuckled, touching a tentative finger to her lips. "I must be a sight."

"I don't think it's safe for anyone to be around me!" Jay stood and pounded around the mat, crying in anguish.

"Shut your pie hole!" Lindy shouted. Jay stopped and looked at the woman on the floor. "Help me up."

She held her hand up, and Jay took it. As she came to her feet, she stumbled forward, caught Jay off-balance and flipped the girl onto her back. Air exploded from Jay's lungs when she landed, and she groaned.

"When you strike you are faster than thought, but you still need to be able to defend yourself."

...please return to the Peacekeeper...

"We better get cleaned up. Training is done for today. You did well, Jay. You're building strength, although, according to Ankh, you'll never be disgustingly bulky like Rivka or me."

"He didn't mean that! I think you are both beautiful." Jay smiled while trying to wipe away some of the blood on Lindy's face.

"I'll wash it off. You didn't even work up a sweat." Lindy showered quickly and then Jay, who maintained a monologue about how much she disliked her curly hair.

"Why is it like that?" Lindy wondered.

"No one seems to know."

"Maybe it's a secret weapon?"

Jay stopped scrubbing it with a towel, contemplated the words, and went back to work on her hair.

When they hurried from the gym Lindy's lips were

almost back to normal, but she kept tentatively poking her face and saying, "Ouch."

Jay tried to apologize, but Lindy wouldn't have it.

"Listen, all of us are enhanced, but I should have healed already. We're bigger and better versions of ourselves, but we still have limits. You have a real superpower. You can move so fast that people can barely see you. The Magistrate? She has a gift, too. Ankh is a genius. Red and me? We're normal people, and glad of the company of those who are special, like you three."

Lindy carefully watched the younger woman for signs of depression. They didn't need someone with super-human speed who was unstable.

Jay nodded. She didn't feel special. She couldn't *feel* her enhancement at all. Her mind willed something to happen, and it did.

Jay shrugged off Lindy's words. "You and Red are the team's power couple. We all wish we had what you two have."

Lindy smiled. "What do you think we have?"

"A partner to share your life with."

"What about that woman from Zaxxon Major?"

Jay blushed as she looked away.

"Come on, now. You've been in touch, haven't you? Maybe give her a call when we get back to the ship. Keep that spark alive."

"She's busy! Lauton is in charge of the whole planet now. They call her 'Premier.'"

"Then she needs someone to talk to who doesn't work for her. I bet she wants to hear from you as much as you want to talk to her. You do, don't you?" Jay nodded. "And you call *us* the power couple. We don't run a planet. Way to go, Jayita!"

Lindy slapped her on the back, and the younger woman stumbled.

"We better hurry," Jay suggested and started to run. Lindy took one more step and Jay was gone.

"That's some crazy shit," Lindy mumbled as she jogged down the corridor toward the hangar bay.

CHAPTER FOUR

Following their new procedure, they Gated to the edge of the system, used their systems to get the tactical picture and make sure they didn't end up in the middle of a hornet's nest, then conducted a shorter Gate jump closer to their destination.

Remus Six.

Chaz flew the corvette to the planet and took the ship in.

Rivka met with the others in *Peacekeeper's* recreation room, galley, common room—the one room that was all things.

"Tell us what happened when you were last here, Red."

"I arrived on a freighter, having been hired by a Blokite named Tod Mackestray. I tried searching the net for him, but nothing came up. I liked that. In my line of work, there's a great deal of value in anonymity. In any case, he had asked me to come to an office in the middle of the capital city of Remulon.

"The office had nothing in it but a desk. The walls were

bare. There was no chair for the guests. He sat on a crate, but if you've ever seen a Blokite, they don't fit in normal chairs. It didn't make any difference to me, but the surroundings were one of those things you think about later as something that should have set off alarms. I didn't know what his line of work was, though, and I was already on the clock. When getting paid, don't ask questions. I let him do all the talking."

Red stared at the wall, losing himself as he thought back to that time. The muscles in his jaw worked as he thought less than fondly of the meeting he was trying to describe.

"He said his trade was influence. I was to do as I was told without question. I tried to clarify that I provided personal protection. I should have balked when he replied, "That, too," but I needed the money. The only credits I had were the ones he had paid me. I owed him.

"He conducted no work in his office. I had to sit outside as if I were a receptionist, but he was paying me top credits, and he gave me a sweet blaster." Red smiled.

"What happened to the blaster?" Rivka asked. Red's smile turned into a frown.

"I threw it in a river and ran from K'Twillis' gang. That wasn't much later, but let me finish with Mackestray." Red looked at the ceiling as he continued to narrate his story. "The first time we left was to meet with one of the candidates for city mayor. Once again, I was outside and didn't hear what they talked about. From that meeting, we went to the guy's opponent, some female. She refused to meet with him privately, so I stayed close by. That was when I learned what he did, but even that didn't seem untoward. All kinds of people try to influence elections.

"It was what came next that brought it all into focus. Mackestray could find nothing on the guy, so he had no leverage, as he explained it. He would have to resort to intimidation. She paid him a bundle. I didn't hear the final number, but it was well into six figures. When we left, we went to the guy's apartment. The Blokite and I waited for him in the hallway. When he arrived, he was angry and threatened to call the police. I roughed him up a little." Red hung his head and let out a long breath. "I held him once he was more pliable, and that was when Mackestray shoved a blade between the guy's ribs. He murdered the guy because we had ourselves an honest politician without secrets in a closet who refused to be intimidated.

"We returned to the office, and that was when I quit. I was hired muscle, but I wasn't. I'd shield an employer with my body, but I wasn't going to murder people, even though I just had. In the eyes of the law, I was a murderer. Mackestray seemed to take it in stride. Told me to keep the blaster, which I did.

"Out of money, I immediately fell in with an Aborginian, a humanoid plant. That dude was huge and leafy. It was weird, but his credits were as good as anyone's. I tried to do some research, but he was incognito too. K'Twillis was a ghost, and I wasn't the only bodyguard, so I took that as a good sign. He was into mining. We visited the site where a line of Remans waited to work. They were carrying bodies out one side while ushering in fresh meat from the other. I never saw such a haphazard operation, but the ore was flowing. I could respect that.

"Within days, the mine was playing out and needed to expand along a vein, but there was a village in the way.

K'Twillis offered to pay them off or move them, but they wanted neither. That was when me and the boys went in and forcibly removed the villagers. Within a day, the mining operation had consumed what was their home. When a few of the villagers returned with spears, K'Twillis ordered their disposal. I went out with the group, but tossed my blaster in the river and ran. I wasn't going to be a party to any more murders."

Red sat down heavily. Lindy hugged him from behind, resting her chin on his shoulder.

"Now that you know, you need to charge me for my crimes. I'm sorry, Magistrate."

The law ran through Rivka's mind. Red had committed a number of crimes, but she was the judge, jury, and executioner. Her word was final.

"Since you are a trusted informant for the Federation, I agree to your plea deal. For the admission of two misdemeanor trespassing charges, I find you not guilty on all other charges. Double jeopardy prevents you from being tried again for those crimes. That's the end of *your* adjudication, but K'Twillis and Mackestray? Those two have a lot to answer for. Their judgments won't be so light once we find them and get to the truth."

"If I may," Erasmus interrupted. Ankh remained stoic throughout. He probably hadn't heard a word Red had said. "How did Mackestray find skeletons in his targets' closets?"

Red turned to the Crenellian, unsure if he was talking to Ankh or the AI in Ankh's head. He decided that it didn't matter. "He was always talking to someone called 'Margaret.'"

"Did you see her?"

"No. It was over a private comm channel with a device he carried."

"I suspect Margaret is an AI. Did he have a spaceship?"

"I don't know. I didn't work for him long enough to find out."

"I'll assume that he does. Someone in his position needs to be able to move quickly and freely. I'll begin my search for a ship that travels where he does. Maybe this won't be so hard after all."

"It won't be that easy," Red suggested. Rivka nodded her agreement.

"I guess our first stop is the mayor," Rivka said. "You said that even the clients became victims, so she is probably still on the hook somehow. Chaz! Get us an appointment. The Magistrate is in the house."

With his usual efficiency, the AI ordered a vehicle with a driver and made an appointment with the mayor's office, since it wasn't possible to make an appointment with the mayor directly. Rivka decided it was better than nothing. The group boarded the small van, the bodyguards in full combat gear. After the last few cases, it was clear that the Magistrate and her team had a huge target on their backs.

She wondered how many times she would be shot while doing her job. She wondered about Grainger and the others. He had said it was dangerous but hadn't expounded.

"What do you think, Red?" Rivka asked.

"Are we taking bets on who bleeds first, how far we end up running, or which bones get broken?" he asked as if reading her thoughts.

"Am I that transparent?"

"We're going into the lion's den, where only lions live. I'm calling first blood today," Red replied nonchalantly.

"I thought *I* had today," Lindy declared. "You have to pick a time."

"Ladies first." Red dipped his head but maintained a constant vigil, watching outside the vehicle.

"By three in the afternoon."

"Fine. I'll take six."

"No!" Rivka shot back. "There will be no blood today."

"No blood today, but running on the next planet? I say it happens within two hours of leaving the ship," Jay offered.

"What?" Rivka glanced from face to face. "Ankh? What do you have to say?"

"Erasmus and I calculate that at least four members of the crew will be injured and all members of the crew will run at some point during this mission."

"It's a case," Rivka clarified. "Four injured and everyone running? I can't believe how little faith you have in the Federation's legal system."

Ankh looked up at the Magistrate, his goggles firmly in place on his forehead. "It has nothing to do with faith and everything to do with statistics and what can be calculated. Calling this a case is a disservice to the real cases out there," Ankh replied evenly. "We are on a mission to find Red's former employers and convince them to do something that they have no intention of doing. When they see

Red, every resource at their command will be brought to bear with the singular intent of killing him. Anyone nearby will be collateral damage." Ankh pointed to those in the van.

"It seems to me," Jay suggested, "that maybe we want to maintain a lower profile. Go undercover."

"You should listen to her," Ankh said. "Her recommended course of action will reduce our casualties by half."

"Aren't you the pleasant one." Rivka snorted. "What's it worth to get in on this?"

"We had to roll over from Collum Gate, but it's a two fifty buy-in. Eight seconds, Magistrate. It was eight whole seconds from when we left the space terminal to first blood. Even Ankh, cynic that he is, had guessed it would take four hours."

"I'm not a cynic. My estimates are based on probabilities, which are rooted in math. I'm very good at math."

"There's two grand in there right now."

Lindy gave the thumbs up.

"I could use that money," Jay admitted.

"Two thousand credits?" Rivka couldn't believe that her team was betting on aspects of the case. "What's the bet that I get the perp?"

"There's no bet on that since it is a hundred percent certain that you will." Red nodded vigorously in support of his own statement.

"I recuse myself completely. You four will have to work it out among yourselves. I can't be betting on when someone gets punched in the face."

"We should add that," Jay suggested.

"Ankh?" Lindy asked.

"Yes, yes. I'll add that as a prop bet. Check your data-pads for the update."

Rivka shook her head. The driver seemed oblivious to the banter. Rivka wished she had been excluded as well. Sometimes it was better not to know.

"If you want to get me anything for Christmas, I'll take ignorance."

"What's Christmas?" Ankh asked.

"Does it come in a spray?" Red wondered.

"I'll take two if anyone finds it," Jay added.

"I feel like the world has turned on its head in the past five minutes." Rivka continued to shake her head until the van pulled in front of the gleaming multi-story building with a massive sign out front that declared it the seat of the Remulon government. By the people and for the people.

Rivka took in the words. Red was the first out of the van, blocking the view of the Magistrate's door with his body. Ankh and Jay climbed out next and walked ahead. Rivka stepped out and followed Red as he took the lead on his way to the entrance. Lindy jumped out last and assumed a position at a reasonable stand-off distance. Her eyes darted back and forth and up and down in a never-ending search pattern.

Red walked quickly but varied his speed, zigzagging on occasion to foil the aim of any sniper.

They breathed a collective sigh of relief when they walked inside, and Rivka glared at her oversized bodyguard.

"What happened to the good old days where we didn't have to walk on pins and needles?"

"I don't remember any days like that. All I remember is

shooting and running, or running and not shooting. Have I mentioned lately how much I love my railgun? Thanks for hooking me up," Red remarked.

"Doesn't look like the home team appreciates it." Rivka held out her credentials as a group of armed security, weapons drawn, rushed toward them. Rivka wondered if Lindy was going to win the first blood bet. Rivka decided it was time to change the dynamic. "I am a Federation Magistrate, and you will stand down!"

The group spread out, slowed, and assumed firing stances, both hands on their handheld weapons as they aimed at the group.

"What the hell did I just say?" Rivka stormed up to the oldest member of the group and shoved her credentials in front of his face. "I suggest you lower your weapons, or the Federation will come down on you like a metric butt-ton of bricks."

The man whipped out a hand and ripped the credentials from Rivka. She could feel her temperature rise and started to shake with anger. The man flipped the badge and document at her face before telling his people to stand down.

Rivka let the credentials bounce off her and land on the floor. When his weapon had been lowered, she launched her fist into his face, snapping his head backward. He was out cold before he hit the floor. "That's for assault and battery on a Federation official, specifically me. You have been judged, asswipe. Paperwork to follow."

He never heard the judgment that was passed. Whenever he woke up, he'd discover that he was a criminal.

"I didn't have time to bet on the punch!" Jay whispered

loudly. Ankh shook his big head, which always made it look like he was going to fall over.

"That line will have to be to the minute. No day or hour bets. Too broad," Ankh declared.

"Focus, people," Red warned. He and Lindy had no time for casual conversation. Their railguns remained leveled at the security personnel.

"Where's the mayor's office?" Rivka demanded.

"Top floor."

"Déjà vu all over again." Rivka waved for the others to follow.

"You can't go up there like that," one of the security people stated, holding his hand out as if that would stop Red.

"What is it with these places? It's like they all have the same playbook." Rivka fixed the man with a withering glare. "You! Shut your pie hole. Magistrate. Under Federation orders. This fuckstick right here, should he ever wake up, is why we're armed. People like you make it necessary for people like me to have people like them!" Rivka stabbed a finger at Red. "Come on."

She headed for the steps without looking back, hearing the footfalls of her team, each distinct and unique, behind her. "Maybe first time someone points a weapon," Jay whispered.

"That seems appropriate, but we'll have to measure that one in seconds," Ankh replied softly. Red picked Ankh up halfway up the first flight of stairs.

Lindy waited at the bottom, covering the security people while the others quickly climbed.

"I think we need to work on our undercover skills," Jay suggested.

At the top of the stairs, Rivka stopped. "No more talk of bets, please. I need to concentrate, because we need the mayor to tell us what we want to know, and then we need to get the hell out of here before someone gets hurt."

"Couldn't agree more, Magistrate," Red replied. "The Blokite will be on the move. Every second we delay is that much more of a lead we give him."

"My thoughts exactly," Rivka agreed. Red put Ankh down, and Jay took the Crenellian's hand. The big man walked carefully to the double doors labeled with the mayor's office coat of arms and slowly opened the door before leading the team through.

CHAPTER FIVE

The outer office was a beehive of activity. No one bothered to look at the visitors until someone noticed the armed party, then, with a gasp and stifled cry, all work ground to a halt. Rivka marched ahead, showing her credentials.

"I'm Magistrate Rivka Anoa, and I need to talk with the mayor. This is Federation business, and I'll tolerate no interference."

The first person to speak didn't make a good impression. "You can't see the mayor."

"Is she not in? Because I think she's here." Rivka looked at Ankh, who nodded slightly.

"You don't have an appointment, and she's busy, so you can't get an appointment." The woman behind the desk didn't bother to stand as she delivered her well-practiced line.

"Red, break the door down."

Like a freight train heading down the tracks, Red launched himself at the door, kicking it handle-high. It burst open. Inside, a naked mayor and well-built young man ducked for cover. Rivka powered in with Jay and Ankh in tow. "Wait here and keep them outside," the Magistrate told Lindy.

Red did a quick survey of the room before grabbing the man by the back of the neck, frog-marching him to the door, and throwing him outside. He pushed the broken door as far closed as it could go, comfortable that Lindy stood just outside. He took the opposite position inside and leaned back to watch Rivka do her job.

Holding a shirt protectively over herself, the mayor snarled and spit invectives.

"Shut up," Rivka ordered. "I know you paid Tod Mackestray to guarantee that you'd win the election. That's quite illegal, I'll have you know. The Federation is a champion of fair and impartial voting processes, so I can either haul your ass off to Jhiordaan, or you can tell me where to find Mackestray."

The woman turned her back while she dressed. After she finished, she slumped into her chair.

"You're in big trouble with the Federation, besides whatever the hell we just witnessed going on in here." Rivka impatiently paced. "Where is he?"

"I haven't heard from him since the election. I am just a mayor, so maybe I'm a nobody to someone like him."

"What did you pay him? Half a mil, was it?" Rivka pressed while she worked her way around the desk to loom over the mayor. "Where is he?" She grabbed the woman's arm and opened her mind, but the mayor didn't know. She wasn't sure where he'd gone after she had won.

She was happy not to have heard from him. But he went somewhere…

"You saw him leaving on a small spaceship. A yacht. Where was it headed?"

Surprise crossed the mayor's face before she resumed her neutral politician's expression.

"The ship's name was *Pandora's Pleasure.* I don't know where it was headed because I didn't want to know. When you become associated with a creature like Tod Mackestray, the less you know, the better off you'll be." She looked at Red. "Haven't I seen you before?"

"I also was an associate of Mister Mackestray for a very brief time," Red admitted.

Ankh disappeared into his own world as he worked with Erasmus to locate the Blokite's yacht.

Wry mirth sparkled in the mayor's expression. She leaned back and closed her eyes. "It wasn't worth it."

"Looks like you were making the best of it," Rivka said pointing with her chin at the clothes still on the floor.

"Well, there *are* some benefits to being me, but overall, I lost my ass and part of my soul. If you can get Mackestray, that would be a great burden lifted from my shoulders."

"That's because he's the causal link to your crimes that we know you've committed." Rivka held the mayor's arm to make sure she understood what the Magistrate was about to say. "I will reserve passing judgment on you—for now, that is. Here's what I need you to do if you are to avoid exposure and punishment. You will be the best damn mayor this city has ever seen. You will be so selfless that homeless people will feel sorry for you."

"I understand," she replied softly.

"That is a far cry from what I need to hear." The images flashing through Rivka's mind suggested she would comply, at least as much as her nature allowed.

"I will do as you require of me."

"You will do as *your people* require. And no more of this bullshit!" Rivka kicked at the clothes as she walked away. Red pulled the door open until it fell off its battered hinges, then leaned it against the wall and shrugged.

Jay took Ankh's hand, and they walked out together. Lindy led the way through the suddenly crypt-quiet group of aides and assistants. The mayor started yelling people's names, creating a stir and a flurry of activity as those called hurried to her office. The naked man was nowhere to be seen. Rivka couldn't complain about the mayor's taste, only her judgment.

And the fact that she was a politician. On the stairs, she asked Jay, "Do you think I'm overly harsh toward politicians?"

"I think politicians are too used to people blowing smoke up their asses. I believe they are genetically incapable of telling the whole truth, so they don't know how to deal with you. You are boxing, and they are trying to play chess. They keep trying to move their pieces while you're punching them in the face. They are left bloodied, not understanding why they haven't won."

"I appreciate your insight. I think they should give you points for the first face punch."

"I think so!"

"No can do," Ankh said.

. . .

Licensing Board Chairman Dies in Fiery Hover Crash

K'Twillis read the headlines twice before digging into the article. "Who's your replacement?" he asked after finding that the board was in limbo. That served his purpose as much as having someone in his pocket. He only needed the pits to work without oversight for a couple more months before he'd cash out and abandon it all.

Coming from a planet of swamps, K'Twillis found that strip mining the drylands for their most profitable minerals wasn't a conflict. If they were decent creatures, then they wouldn't live in such climates. He reasoned that he could do nothing to their already ugly planets that would make them worse.

Except line his pockets, if he'd had pockets.

What does the galaxy's richest mining entrepreneur do with his money?

"Whatever I want," he answered himself. "I will stop when I can buy an entire planet. I need enough people to keep my swamp clean, to keep the skies clear, and make sure that no one bothers me. That is my desire." He stood alone in a channel of water well away from the city. He didn't need the modern conveniences the population embraced. He needed money, lots of expendable credit chips, and a few phone numbers. Outside of that, he trusted the planetary surveys done by a Magnetite trader, for which K'Twillis paid him well.

Finding key people was easy. Getting them to turn a blind eye was almost as simple most of the time, but on Felgar, he found his efforts repulsed. That was why the chairman had to die. If he had to remove another, people would grow suspicious and the tendrils leading back to him would become more prevalent.

He wanted only enough time to finish the job and move on. Anonymity was his friend.

"Billister!" he "shouted" through his microphone.

The wiry former soldier appeared, eyes shifting with each step. The ease with which he carried his weaponry suggested the man knew one purpose in life.

"Sir?" Billister's voice sounded like gravel bouncing within a can. K'Twillis' ears couldn't tell the difference.

"Prepare primary and contingency plans to eliminate the members of the licensing board."

"Roger," the man confirmed before walking out.

"You make this easy," K'Twillis called. He contemplated paying the man a bonus but rejected it. He was already being paid top credit. Pay for the best, get the best. Now, if only the miners would pick up the pace. "Billister! Tomorrow morning we're taking a trip to the pit. You might have to light a fire under those lazy bastards. Are your boys ready and able to do that?"

"Lighting a fire" was the harshest phrase the Aborginian could use. On his planet, no good came from fire. It was beyond deadly to his people.

Billister stuck his head back in the door. "Of course. I'll line up the truck. Four AM departure to catch them sleeping on the job?"

It wasn't the first time they'd visited the site. It definitely wouldn't be the last. The security man knew that the time frame allocated for the operation was shrinking, which meant more hands-on engagement. If the workers would work only when the whip was cracked, then they'd have to score a great number of backs to get the job done.

Billister was fine riding herd on the minions. He earned one month of vacation a year, working twenty-four/seven the other eleven months. This was the other eleven. He checked his mental whip to make sure the spurs and burrs were in place and ready to tear flesh.

"Come on, boys, we have a couple missions," he told the group of locals he'd hired solely for their muscles and lack of attachments. In the end, they'd all be killed. He couldn't leave loose ends hanging, like the one who got away. He'd never forget the man's name.

Vered.

"Where are we going, Ankh?" Rivka asked.

The Crenellian stared unfocused eyes at a spot on the bulkhead. "Erasmus has tracked the ship through three different destination systems. The newest information is months old, unfortunately, but maybe that indicates Tod Mackestray and *Pandora's Pleasure* are still there."

"Sounds like a shortcut. Take us out, Chaz," Rivka ordered while she studied the screen. "Look at the election cycle on that planet. I'm willing to bet that the elections happened a couple of months ago."

"You are correct," Erasmus noted. "Extrapolating election data and overlaying it on the star chart, focusing solely on planet-wide events, we have three potential systems where Mackestray may currently be."

"Do we guess, or do we go to his last known location

and try to find out what he renamed his ship?" Rivka asked rhetorically.

Jay put her hand on the Magistrate's shoulder to show her camaraderie with the unanswerable. "Whatever we do, you'll make it work."

"Last known location," Rivka declared. "I'm still building the case. I want to interrogate the accused to learn the truth. I believe Red unequivocally, but I need this to be airtight. When we have Mister Mackestray in custody, we'll go back to those we've talked to and make sure he's the one, if there is any doubt whatsoever."

"I hope it turns out that way, Magistrate," Red replied. "I think it'll probably end with the sound of railguns unloading."

"I get the impression he won't go without a fight. I don't want to take unnecessary risks to capture him alive."

"The universe will be a much better place without someone like Tod Mackestray in it," Red remarked.

"I can't make that judgment right now. I hope you understand." Rivka noted the sour expressions, but she couldn't compromise her principles.

Red nodded, tight-lipped.

"First and foremost, we need to have the bounty removed. Ankh, is there anything you can do about that?"

Ankh's vacant expression suggested he was elsewhere.

"Erasmus? What can you do about removing any references to a price on Red's head?"

"Finding such a thing is a significant challenge. Where do criminals hide their crimes? Which bars do hitmen frequent, and what do they post to be discovered later? I fear that there is no way for me to resolve the issue digitally. It will take removing the source for the payment."

"Do you have anything that says for certain there is a contract out on Red?"

"The only thing in Federation possession is images of flyers found in various dives showing a picture of Vered and a variety of reward credits."

"What's the highest?" Red asked.

"Fifty thousand," Erasmus replied over the ship's speakers.

Red looked disappointed.

"That's a rather hefty sum for someone to push you out an airlock," Rivka suggested. Lindy gave Red a push from behind.

"Fifty k?"

"Stop it." Red smiled and pushed her back. "I'm still not sure what I'm getting paid since the deposit amounts seem to vary wildly. Are you deducting for ammunition used?"

Rivka shrugged and threw up her hands. "How would I know any of that? I don't know what *I'm* getting paid. I think what you really want to know, my rather large friend, is whether it is more lucrative to keep you around."

"Inquiring minds want to know. Do I have to sleep with one eye open?" Red looked at Lindy, head up and eyes narrowed in question.

"Since I don't want any felons on my crew, I guess we'll issue the edict that no one gets to kill Red to collect the credits. The Magistrate has spoken. So let it be written, so let it be done!" Rivka pounded one fist on the table.

"Why not?" Jay asked.

"What?" Rivka and Red asked together.

"You always say to follow the money. Maybe we kill Red and then demand payment. I don't mean really kill him, just make it look good enough to be paid for our services. Ankh can trace the money and maybe help us find who we're looking for. There are two contracts, so maybe we can kill two birds with one stone." Jay crossed her arms and smirked.

"Two birds and Red. Sounds like a banner day," Lindy noted with a laugh. "And it sounds like a great plan."

Rivka started pacing, hands behind her back as the details to support Jay's idea rushed into her head. "Undercover, where we reduce our exposure and get them to come to us. I believe these used to be called 'sting operations.'"

"So much better than punching people in the face," Jay suggested without making eye contact with the Magistrate.

"If there is no face punching or blood, then no one wins the pool." Rivka stopped pacing to look at her team.

"The credits roll over. There will be blood eventually. Someone will win. Grainger expressed interest in joining the pool, as did the other Magistrates." Red helped himself to five food bars from the processor before asking if anyone else wanted something.

"They wouldn't dare!"

"I'll take their money," Lindy said. Jay nodded. She would, too.

"Ankh? Are you with us, buddy?" Rivka asked.

"He is occupied presently, but we like your plan. Wherever we go next, we'll need someone to be the executioner. That someone needs to be either Jay or Lindy. You can't do it, Magistrate, and Ankh refuses to play that role. He chooses to remain aboard *Peacekeeper*."

"I'll do it," Jay said.

"I'm probably more credible," Lindy refuted.

Rivka was torn. She didn't want to put either woman in the line of fire, although one could dodge bullets, while the other would survive getting hit.

"Where's a man I can offer up for sacrifice?" Rivka pondered. No one laughed. "I'm sorry, Jay."

"Does that mean it is or isn't me?"

"I guess it depends on how you look at it. I'm going with Lindy for this. It's your idea, but I need you to cover Ankh. He, as we have learned in this fantastic future where we live, is critical to finding the evidence we need to locate and prosecute the perpetrators."

"Glorious," Red interjected through a mouthful of food bar.

"I know you like the new food bars. You can thank Ankh later."

Red swallowed heavily. "No, I want my *death* to be glorious! Explosions and fire, railguns echoing, people screaming, children crying, and burly, manly men raising buckets of ale in my honor. It's the least you can do for me, Magistrate. Maybe pay me time-and-a-half for my troubles?"

"You and your damn credits. What do you spend your money on, anyway?"

"I have people to take care of now. I'm saving for a month-long honeymoon."

Lindy smiled.

"Sorry to burst your bubble, but we're just going to

transmit a phony death certificate. I think you'll die in your sleep from poison that gave you a heart attack. The poison will have been hidden in a raspberry chocolate flambeau."

Red's lip curled in disgust. "I will never be able to show my face in public again."

"That's the idea." Rivka patted his cheek before returning to the bridge. "Erasmus, we have to make some plans and bring Ankh along with you..."

CHAPTER SIX

Tod Mackestray sat on the bench in a space that served as the dining room and living room. The Blokite's space yacht was built for speed and maneuverability, along with enough creature comforts for no more than two people. Best if the two were a couple since there was only one bed.

He didn't have a partner. That bothered him, but not enough to do anything about it. He didn't trust anyone enough to let them share his life. He would always suspect that they were after his money.

"Margaret, what's the ETA to our next target? I mean planet? I mean conquest?" The Blokite laughed at his own joke.

"We are fifteenth in the queue through this Gate. There is only a short wait at the second Gate, making our estimated time of arrival in nine hours."

"What is it going to take to get a Gate drive and one of the new Federation power sources?"

"That is restricted technology and only installed on official Federation ships. Should such a vessel be captured, the AI will suicide, taking the technology with it. At this point in time, I don't see a way to acquire the drive or power source."

"Keep your ear to the stars. They'll come available, and when they do, I want to be the first to get one. I don't care about the cost."

"Your wish is my command," Margaret replied.

"Just how I like it."

Tod Mackestray retired to the bed.

"Let me know when we arrive, Margaret. I'm sure I'll be busy since the elections aren't far off."

The cycling of the Gate engine was nearly silent, but the shift through the Etheric dimension announced their arrival at the edge of Leed's Planet space—a single habitable planet in a three-planet system orbiting a large K-Class star.

"No unusual chatter. No noise at all," Chaz reported. "No obvious threats."

"Take us in soon as you can."

"Counting down from ten minutes until the Gate engines are recharged."

"Thanks, Chaz."

Rivka left the bridge and joined the others in the recreation room. "We're going to kill you when we land, Red," Rivka stated matter-of-factly. "The elections here seem like they didn't go well. There was an inordinate amount of mud-slinging, which may or may not indicate Mackestray was here. Was it business as usual? I can't tell when it comes to politicians."

Jay shook her head. "It's too easy to believe the worst things."

"We'll see whoever is in charge and work our way backward from there. Ankh?"

The Crenellian looked at the Magistrate through bloodshot eyes.

"When was the last time you slept?"

"I don't need sleep like humans. You people embrace your slices of death as if they are magical. I'll never understand it."

"You look tired as hell. You should get some rest. We'll be there soon."

"Is that what you wanted?" Ankh asked.

"No, sorry. Once we're on the ground, I need you to find out what happened to *Pandora's Pleasure*."

"Erasmus is already on that. He'll be accessing the appropriate databases as soon as we arrive."

"Accessing appropriate databases," Rivka said slowly. "In my reports, I reference your cyber-sleuthing as those things discovered via a digital footprint. Do I want to know the details of how you find the information?"

Ankh held her gaze as he answered, "You do not."

"At some point in time, we may have to testify regarding how we did it. Defend that we had probable cause to search."

"That sounds like a waste of time. I hate wasting time. We will not testify."

"You might have to."

"No, we don't."

"But you might have to," Rivka reiterated.

"No, we don't. How long are we going to do this, Magistrate? I have programs I need to work on."

"I guess we're done—for now, that is. Just in case, make sure you..." Rivka's voice trailed off.

"Do you want the information or not? Our methods are from original programming that most people wouldn't understand. Ted understands, and Plato, of course, but not your average human."

"It's hard not to take that personally, Ankh." Rivka laughed and smiled. "But it is exactly what you mean because it's true, even though I think we have vastly different definitions of average."

Ankh didn't respond.

"When we hit the ground, Lindy, Jay, and I will head into town. Red, even though you're dead, stay frosty. We may need you, but your first job is to keep Ankh safe."

Red nodded and held out his hand. Rivka took what he offered—the coin-sized devices that Ankh had made to help him access alien computer systems.

She immediately shoved them into a jacket pocket.

"I might have forgotten those, but I doubt it," Rivka muttered.

"I have mine!" Jay held hers up. Lindy dug into a pocket and pulled out two as well.

"Is this a conspiracy?" Rivka raised one eyebrow with her question.

"It's your team looking out for you," Red suggested, his face serious. "We have everything to lose if you fail."

Rivka's eyes glistened for a moment before she blinked. "Thank you. Not the least of which is getting killed."

"I'll take one for the team, but space herpes, of all things?" Red stated, earning himself a punch in the arm.

"Maybe I *will* kill you and collect the reward. Space herpes? That implies I gave it to you. I will not be besmirched. Where's my railgun?"

Red and Lindy wrestled briefly until their lips found each other. Jay and Rivka turned away. Ankh looked to be asleep.

"Gate engine is active. Gate formed. Gravitic shields are nominal. Accelerating over the event horizon."

An instant later, *Peacekeeper* materialized above Leed's Planet. Chaz requested approach instructions and was instantly granted approval with a direct flight path to the capital city's spaceport.

"No waiting. Maybe they were expecting us." Rivka returned to the cockpit. Even if they had been expected, things were never that smooth. Red and Lindy followed her. "Show the tactical picture, Chaz."

"There is a distinct lack of vessels in orbit. Planet communications are minimal. There are no public video or audio broadcasts."

"How advanced is this planet? Shouldn't there be something?"

"We are being vectored by an automated system. The landing pad is clear. Should I set down?"

"Sure. Something feels off, but we're not going to figure it out from inside the ship."

"Landing now. I have not been able to secure a vehicle, but I will keep trying."

Rivka found Lindy in full gear. Jay looked like she was dressed for a day of shopping. "I need you to put on your vest," Rivka told her as she reached for her own body armor to wear under her jacket.

"You think it's going to be that dangerous?" Jay asked.

"I never think that, but Red has taught me to adopt a certain level of paranoia. Our cases have reinforced that perspective. So yes, put on your gear, and let's go to town. Ankh? I think it's about time to let Erasmus kill our esteemed colleague. It has been a great run, Red. Sorry you died."

A boom shook the ship. "Chaz?" Rivka called while hurrying back to the bridge. "Tactical!"

"It appears that we are under attack. A mortar projectile has landed nearby. More are inbound."

"Get us out of here," Rivka ordered.

"A number of Ledonians have taken refuge beneath the ship. If we leave, they'll be exposed."

"Standby." Rivka found Red behind her. "Don't kill Red! We've got some work to do first. Suit up, and tell Lindy to get ready to drive the mech suit."

"Yeeha!" Red hooted. His gear was never far away, and in less than a minute, he was armed and ready to go. "Helmet on," he told Jay.

"I'm not sure I want to go out there at all." Jay retreated to the wall and leaned against it with her arms crossed.

"Erasmus, can you tell what the hell is going on out there?"

"I've been analyzing the information since we reached orbit and have come to a startling conclusion."

Rivka waited for Erasmus to continue, which he did after the appropriate dramatic pause.

"We've landed in the middle of a civil war."

Rivka frowned and started to rub her temples. "I didn't think they were shooting at us just to shoot at us, although that's not too far-fetched. We still need the information they have somewhere on this damn planet, and that means we need to go find it. Lindy, load up in the mech. Red, I, and yes, you too, Jay are heading into town. We're going to count on Jay's newfound speed to help us get where we need to go. We'll count on the mech's firepower in case the locals don't want to let us through. And Erasmus, make sure you report your findings to the Federation. I think they'll want to know."

Lindy reluctantly put her weapons on the table, slapping a hand blaster onto her belt to carry inside the suit.

"Once Lindy has the mech powered up and detached, I'll come for you," Red remarked. He checked his helmet one last time before looking Lindy over. She had her protective gear on to help unhook the mech, but she'd have to shed it before getting inside the suit. She was going to be exposed more than anyone was comfortable with.

But it had to be done, because criminals had put a price on Vered's head, and no one was good with that.

Red's hand hovered over the button to open the hatch. He nodded toward the Magistrate, who took out her neutron pulse weapon nicknamed Reaper and stood ready to secure the ship after the two were outside.

Explosions continued to buffet the ship. The gravitic shields were functioning, but while sitting on the ground, they didn't provide optimal protection.

"Sounds nasty out there," Rivka said unnecessarily.

"We'll stop that bullshit as soon as Lindy is in the suit."

Red mashed the button, and the hatch opened and

dropped the stairs to the ground. He headed out first and instantly started yelling, "Get the fuck back!" He fired his railgun into the air. "Get back!" A few more rounds and he was heading toward the ground with Lindy close behind.

Rivka closed the hatch and ran to the bridge, where Chaz was monitoring the situation outside the ship. Red was holding back those taking cover under the ship while Lindy started to climb to the top where the suit had been secured. After a growl and a feint, he jumped to the hand-holds and pulled himself up.

Lindy released the main clamps, which exposed the rear access. It was like the zipper on a full-body suit. There wasn't much room inside, so she had to worm her way through the opening, breathing a sigh of relief once she was able to power up the suit and close it around her. Red kneeled nearby and fired at random targets to give Lindy the time she needed to run through the start-up sequence. "Point of order," she told the suit. "We need a way to power up the suit and do all this remotely."

"I will see what I can do to make that happen," Erasmus replied through her internal speakers.

"You can hear me?"

"I think you already know the answer."

"Am I linked to anyone else?"

"No. I tapped in as soon as you powered up the system. Use your internal comm chip so everyone can hear you. You'll be leading, since the groups fighting do not have sufficiently advanced weapons to cause much damage to the suit."

"I'm not sure whether that's a good thing or not. 'Much damage' seems relative. On the other hand, maybe there is hope that these factions aren't fighting a war that would destroy their planet."

She continued through the start-up sequence. When all the lights were green, she unbolted the last restraints and stood up.

What do you say we stop being targets? Lindy asked.

Maybe you can send a rocket to say 'Hi!' to that mortar. He's pissing me off, Red replied.

Lindy accessed the heads-up display, the HUD, and selected one of the four rockets mounted over her shoulder. She dialed in the mortar's position, which the suit had automatically calculated based on the trajectory of the incoming fire. With a whoosh, the rocket was away.

Moments later, a massive explosion signaled the end of the attack on the ship.

Lindy lifted Red, took two steps, and jumped. She laughed as they fell, activating the micro-rockets on the bottom of her boots to slow her descent right before they hit the ground. Those hiding under the ship jumped back to avoid getting crushed.

Open the hatch. The coast is clear.

Erasmus uploaded a map to Lindy's HUD.

Red stomped his foot and yelled, "Get away from here!" The Ledonians, a humanoid species covered in short brown fur, waved their weapons at him and chattered something his chip couldn't translate. "Don't make me kill you."

He fired a single projectile from his railgun, and the hypervelocity crack as it passed between them made them scream and hold their heads in pain. He shouted and menaced them until they ran off.

Rivka and Jay joined Red and Lindy, taking stock of the area around the ship. Quiet had returned.

"Spooky," Jay commented. "Big cities are supposed to be noisy."

Rivka accessed her datapad.

Red was instantly miffed. "You couldn't have done that inside the ship?"

She ignored him, knowing that he was right. "Ankh," she started, "this changes the dynamic. I'm assuming the main government building is ground zero in one way or another. Where will we find the information?"

I suggest you go to the National Data Center, which is four kilometers north-northeast. I've sent the directions to Lindy as well.

Taking the lead and moving out, Lindy declared. *Stay behind me.*

Which was what Red usually said, but he was under no illusion regarding his own survivability compared to the mech. The rhythmic thumping of the mech suit as Lindy walked gave him comfort. The impact tremors represented power.

Rivka held out her hand and snapped her fingers, but no one reacted. "Give me the other railgun!"

Red shrugged. "I don't have it."

"Don't tell me..." Rivka looked at the top of *Peacekeeper.*

"We left it inside."

"Whew. That's right. Lindy disarmed before you went outside."

"You okay, Magistrate?" Red asked without looking at her. He studied both sides of their route, finding that he had to jog to keep up. Jay ran behind the mech, while Red and Rivka ran side by side behind her.

"Just bothered. How could the Federation not know the planet had devolved into a civil war?"

"No idea. But I bet Tod Mackestray had something to do with it."

"You hate that guy. I'm not sure I'd give him all the credit. For people to do this, the fuel has to already be there. He may have provided the spark, but it was already smoldering."

"Who's responsible?" Red wondered, "the fuel, or the one who starts the fire?"

"I hope we become enlightened, or we're running eight clicks for no reason."

"Running. Dammit! Ankh wins the pool."

Barricade up ahead, Lindy reported. *It's manned, and they have rifles.*

Her words arrived a millisecond before the first cracks echoed down the empty roadway. Bullets whistled past, and one tinged off the armored suit. Lindy raised her over-sized railgun. *Light 'em up?* she asked.

Scare them only, Rivka ordered.

Lindy fired at the sides of the barricade, shredding it and sending shrapnel flying. The screams of the injured filled the silence once her fire stopped.

Sorry about that.

"I bet they're plenty scared," Red suggested.

They proved him wrong by firing everything they had. Red grabbed the Magistrate and pulled her to the ground, covering her body with his.

Light 'em up, Rivka passed over her internal comm chip.

Jay crawled toward them and worked her way next to Rivka. Red lay across them both.

Lindy braced herself and walked the railgun fire from one side of the barricade to the other. Then she did it again, quicker the second time. She started running, picking up speed quickly, and sprinted through the wreckage, sliding to a stop on the other side. Her optics and sensors picked up two living among the twenty-five Ledonians, and they were injured. She found them huddled together, moaning with pain and barely conscious.

All clear, she reported. Lindy wondered if she'd grown heartless. Using the argument of "they fired first" was meaningless because they couldn't hurt her, not with their primitive weaponry.

The other three joined her, but she hesitated.

"It sucks," Rivka said softly. "We didn't start this, but if we *can* end it, we will. I know that's not quite the Magistrate's role, but it's what we do for all humanity. We will bring death and destruction the likes of which they've never imagined, or they can stop fighting and start talking."

The thunder of a heavy weapon arrived a millisecond after the shell hit Lindy in her mechanized chest, throwing her over Red's head to land in an unmoving heap. He shouted his war cry and unleashed a steady stream from his railgun at a tank that appeared at the next corner. Rivka hit him with a shoulder block as the second shot screamed past.

She dialed Reaper to eleven and activated it as she aimed at the tank. The tank's barrel adjusted its aim, and Rivka and Red rolled out of the way as the high-velocity round slammed into the ground where they'd just been.

"Run!" Rivka yelled without looking back at the mech.

Lindy? Red ventured as he dodged, looking for cover.

"Dammit! Too far away," Rivka growled when the neutron pulse weapon failed to kill the people inside the tank.

"Too far?" Jay shouted. "We need to help Lindy!"

Before Rivka could move, a blur rushed by, ripping Reaper from her hand and racing down the street. Jay ran past the tank, pointing the weapon at it before skidding to a stop and retracing her steps. She zigzagged as she ran, but the tank stopped moving, the barrel frozen where it had last aimed.

Red raced to Lindy, kneeling over her and trying to see through the reflective face shield. Lindy's eyelids fluttered, and Red's heart started beating again.

"Ow," Lindy mouthed.

Ankh. What can you tell about the suit's systems? Rivka asked.

Multiple failures. Rerouting systems and recalculating optimal power application to minimize impact from the damage.

Life signs? Rivka followed.

She'll be fine. Some broken bones. Well, a lot of broken bones, but they're already healing. That's the power of multiple trips through the Pod-doc, which has made her bulky enough to withstand this amount of damage.

Don't let her hear you say that, Red warned.

It applies. I don't see the problem.

The problem is that Bulky Woman will kick your ass.

"What did you call me?" a mumbled voice projected through the suit's external speakers.

Ankh, I swear I'm going to tape you to the ceiling. Red

smiled as he tried to lift Lindy's head, but he couldn't because the mech suit was too dense.

Terry Henry Walton had a dog taped to his face. It can't be any worse than that, although it would be most undeserved. I think you should probably continue to the data center. This city is unstable. Someone is pounding on the ship's hatch. Standby. There. A mindful jolt of electricity through the outer hull has sent them running for cover. Their hair seems to be smoking. Stop. Drop. Roll. Okay. No taping me to any ceilings or walls. I'm too busy for such childish nonsense.

Ankh. Can you use any of the ship's sensors to give us a tactical picture? I'd like to avoid what we just went through. I don't want to kill anyone else if I don't have to, Rivka requested.

The information is on your datapad and on Lindy's display whenever she's conscious enough to see it.

CHAPTER SEVEN

"Sometimes, Ankh, you can be such an ass," Red muttered under his breath.

Lindy groaned as she sat up. "I feel like I've been run over by a comet."

"Close," Rivka said softly. "We hear you have a few broken bones in there."

That sounds wonderful compared to how I feel. The good old days, when we laughed at a few broken bones. I miss them.

"Sounds like you're on the mend." Red gently caressed the side of the mech's helmet as if Lindy could feel it. They couldn't see her expression behind the reflective setting, but she was smiling.

I'm going to stand up. I guess lying around out here isn't something we want to do too much of.

Red finally looked away and scanned the surroundings. Jay was standing to the side, watching for any movement.

Rivka joined her. Lindy stood and worked out the kinks as her nanocytes repaired the damage to her body. The suit was horribly dented, but the round hadn't penetrated. They didn't want to find out if they could survive such an injury even though they were told they would. No one had been willing to test it.

Lindy took a few tentative steps, followed by a few more. She systematically worked through the flashing lights on the HUD until they turned green.

The suit's structure is compromised. It says it can't withstand another impact in the same area.

"Sounds like you need a shield. Let's find you a healthy chunk of steel," Red said and stalked toward the barricade. The mech pounded the pavement after him.

Rivka joined Jay. "Thanks for saving our asses."

"What good is a gift if you don't use it?" Jay softly kicked debris from the barricade.

"I'm glad you're on my team. Your wisdom belies your youth. There are times when I don't want to touch people because I don't want to know. Then there are times when we're hunting a perp, like now, and I want to grab everyone and shake them until they tell me where he is."

"You're not very intimidating." Jay avoided looking at the bits and pieces of bodies scattered across the ground before them. The screech of tearing metal shocked their senses.

Red stumbled away, his hands locked firmly over his ears as Lindy used the mech's power to bend a metal sheet in half and then in fourths. She twisted one side to create a handle and hoisted the piece in front of her chest. *This will have to do,* she said.

Rivka turned back to Jay. "*I* think I'm intimidating," she replied defensively.

"Red is intimidating. Once you break out your Magistrate creds and start beating the perps, others sit up and take notice."

"Creds and beatings, huh?" Rivka shook her head. "The things I have to do to earn respect. Looks like it's time to go. Next stop? I hope it's the data center. We don't need any more of this crap."

The blown barricade stood as a stark reminder of what they were up against. There was no way to know if they'd run across more. They had always counted on Ankh's ability to penetrate systems, but this was different. This was primitive warfare that left no digital fingerprints.

"If Tod Mackestray was in any way responsible for this, his life is forfeit," Rivka declared as she started to jog after the mech, which was moving with renewed purpose.

Lindy manhandled the oversized railgun with one mechanized arm while she held the ad hoc shield in the other. She walked quickly but with a slight jerk as the servos compensated for the changed weight distribution and the suit's damaged components.

"I can run ahead and see if there are any more obstructions or defenders," Jay offered. Rivka pulled out her datapad as she loped behind the mech. The route was clearly displayed.

"The suit has sensors," Red interrupted.

"That were housed in the chest plate. This suit has no functioning sensors," Lindy replied through the suit's external speakers.

"Be right back," Jay told them.

"I don't doubt that."

In a flash, Jay was gone.

"That is some crazy shit," Rivka mumbled.

"I could use a little of that." Red sauntered up.

"Ankh said it was a trade-off. Speed or bulk. You want to be the skinny guy so I can kick sand in your face just so you can run fast?"

"I was never the skinny guy," Red answered. "Alas, us bulky people will be left behind as the world gets faster."

"Ankh won the pool," Rivka countered Red's jibe.

"That shall forever chap my ass." Red watched the rooftops and balconies as they jogged between buildings that should have been bustling with activity, down roads that should have been packed with vehicles and people. "Can we call this a mission?"

"We're here to collect evidence for our case against Mackestray. Can't have outsiders doing crap like this."

"I don't mind shooting legitimate bad guys, but I don't know what these fuckers are fighting about. Have we chosen a side by shooting up a checkpoint and destroying a mortar?"

"Probably. The fact that they both shot at us first won't matter. I expect we'll end up fighting them all until we fly out of here." Rivka's voice trailed off, and she clenched her jaw as she ran.

"You want to end this war, don't you?" Red asked.

Jay reappeared next to the Magistrate. *The way ahead is clear as long as we make one detour off the main street. At the next block, take a hard right into the alley. Loop around behind the building, up two blocks, and then back onto this road,* she passed over their internal comm so Lindy would hear, too.

Roger, Lindy replied.

"I want the war to end," Rivka answered Red's question.

"If we have the chance, we'll end it, but we're here to find out where Mackestray went."

Lindy started walking away and soon sped up. She followed Jay's instructions as the group ran in silence, keeping their thoughts to themselves. After ten minutes of a quick pace, they arrived at the building that Erasmus had told them was the data center.

"The quiet is creepy as hell," Rivka said.

I don't think the mech will fit through the door, Lindy guessed.

Red was torn. He wanted to stay outside with her, but his first duty was to protect the Magistrate.

Hide the suit outside and join us. We don't know how long we'll be in there, Red suggested.

"Sounds good," Rivka agreed, nodding to the mirrored surface of the mech's helmet visor. Lindy moved to an alcove and parked the mech. The back unzipped, and she climbed out.

"Safed out?" Red asked, using the military term for rendering a system inoperable.

"It won't activate for anyone but us," she replied. Red ran a hand across her ribs.

"Are you okay?"

"Getting better each minute. Without the Pod-doc I'd be dead, wouldn't I?"

"Without having gone through the Pod-doc, you wouldn't be here at all. We are better for you being with us," Rivka stated. She gripped the former waitress' arm. "And with you keeping him in line, the rest of us can do our jobs."

Lindy chuckled. "Fair enough. Maybe we should get out of the open?"

"De-creepify our situation," Jay answered.

"If I only had a railgun," Rivka sang. Red shook his head on his way through the door. Lindy blocked Rivka's body with her own even though she wore no armor. They quickly followed Red inside to find no sounds and nothing to indicate anyone was there.

Rivka accessed her datapad and called Ankh. "You think the computers are in the basement?"

"I don't waste time thinking about things when I have data that gives me an answer. The main data storage is in the basement."

Rivka pursed her lips and berated herself internally for not asking the right question.

"Tell me how best to access the data," she corrected.

"Put one of my coins near the data storage, but if there's no access terminal, then you'll need to find one of those. They could be anywhere."

"Thanks, Ankh." Rivka stuffed her datapad inside her coat. "We need to put a device downstairs while finding an access terminal. Red, with me. Lindy and Jay, stay together and see what you can find."

Red stood as if rooted to the floor.

"Well?" she asked.

"Do you know where the stairs are?"

"What if I did?"

"Then we'd probably be walking toward them," Red answered.

"Fine. We need to locate the steps."

Red headed in one direction and Rivka the other. He

raced after her when he discovered that she wasn't following him. "Wait up, Magistrate."

"We can cover more ground separately," she remarked.

"Or I can open the doors since you aren't armed. What if you find someone who isn't happy that you're in her building? I can't do my job if you're over here and I'm over there."

Rivka nodded and motioned for him to take the lead.

"You give me shit, but if you were any more bullheaded, you'd have horns," Red muttered as he walked past.

"I'm going to think about that, and when I come up with a proper retort, you'll find it waiting for you on your datapad."

Red laughed while he studied the doorways. He stopped and pointed to a sign that read Stairway.

When Rivka was behind him, he opened and ducked his head in. "I'm glad there's still power."

"Do you have your goggles, just in case? Bad luck seems to follow us around, so I expect we'll be down there in the dark."

"Of course. Those things are gold. Bad luck follows us? That's pretty funny, Magistrate."

"What do you mean?"

"In a small pond of clear water, what happens when you jam a stick into the bottom and start swirling it around?"

"I've never done that, so I don't know for sure, but let me guess. The mud and trash rise to the top."

"It has zero to do with luck and everything to do with the stirring."

"Then let's go see what there is to see and start stirring the pond. Let the evidence collection begin."

"Stay behind me, and next time, you really should bring the railgun."

Rivka tried to poke him in the back, but his body armor protected him. Improvised weapons—she used to be good with those when she first started training with Grainger. She kept her eyes peeled for something to use as they descended the wide staircase.

The smooth shine on the flooring suggested that many feet had walked the stairs over the years. It was far different from the data center on Collum Gate.

Checking in. You guys okay? Rivka asked.

All good up here. We've found a few terminals in offices, but nothing that suggests data entry. We're still looking. No sign of Ledonians, Lindy replied.

Red continued to the bottom, where it opened to a wide, well-lit area. Workout equipment filled the interior. A short track ran along the outside walls, circling the area. Machines, free weights, treadmills, stair climbers, and other equipment called to the physically fit. A climbing wall was in the middle of the room with nets and climbing ropes around it. Rivka picked up an empty bar for weight plates to use as a weapon.

"I smell sweat," Rivka said.

"Ten years from now it'll probably still smell of sweat."

"I smell something else, too..." Rivka sniffed and turned in a circle, trying to find the source of the odor.

Red kept his railgun leveled as he moved through the area, ready to light up an enemy should one appear.

"Maybe check in with Mister I Don't Guess about his facts regarding data storage in the basement?"

"Maybe there are two basements," Rivka suggested.

"Maybe the storage facility was never down here." Red changed to his internal comm. *There's a big gym downstairs. We haven't found any electronics whatsoever. Did you find any other stairways?*

There are two staircases that lead up. That's all we've found.

Stay frosty. Things aren't what they seem, Red replied.

"I agree with that," Rivka said, "but I don't know what's wrong. We expected one thing and found another, but that isn't it. There's something else." Rivka closed her eyes and held up her hands as if they were antennae. Red spared an instant to watch but returned to scanning the area. His eyes caught something, and he froze.

"Video surveillance. We're being watched."

Rivka opened her eyes. "It's their building, and it's legal to put in security systems."

"Who puts a security system in an office gym? Look at it. My nine o'clock, about three meters high."

"How do we know someone is monitoring it?"

"We don't," Red replied. He removed a grenade from his vest. "I'm going to take it out."

"With a grenade?"

Red reached back to throw the grenade, and Rivka ran the other way. She didn't see him throw, but she heard the crunch as the grenade hit the equipment. The Magistrate threw herself to the ground and covered her head.

"Bullseye." Red chuckled as he recovered the grenade. He jogged around the perimeter, taking out three other monitors by jumping and butt-stroking them with his railgun.

Rivka sat on the floor taking in Red's efforts. "You could have told me you didn't pull the pin."

"I thought you would have guessed. I have no desire to see how much damage my body can take." Red hesitated, remembering the tank round that had hit Lindy in the chest. He snarled at the thought, his manhood challenged when she protected them all. He had agreed that he wouldn't protect her over the others; that they were all at equal risk and each carried the responsibility to protect the others to the best of their ability.

"Red?" Rivka called, shaking him from his introspection.

"Roger," he answered, looking around quickly to make sure nothing had happened during his brief mental absence. *Focus on the job at hand,* he reminded himself.

It was hard for a man like him to be in love.

"Looks like a door over here." Rivka pointed at the wall and a recessed handle. "I wonder where this goes?"

She reached for the handle, but Red yelled, "Let me do that."

He motioned for her to step away, then pulled the circular handle out and twisted it, popping the wall open. It slowly pulled outward. He peeked into the darkness before dodging back. He pulled his goggles over his eyes and ducked his head in and out before closing the door.

"What? What did you see?"

CHAPTER EIGHT

"It's a locker room."

"Maybe there's another door. Let's go in." Rivka wondered why Red had stepped back. She twirled her finger at him—hurry up.

He pulled it open and stepped back. Rivka stopped at the entrance and let her eyes adjust. Once she could see, she was greeted by women's underwear scattered throughout.

"Looks like there was a freaking orgy." Rivka walked carefully through the area. "This is where that smell was coming from, too. I didn't think you were squeamish. What's up?"

"Lindy leaves her underwear all over the place. How does she have that much stuff?" Red blurted.

"I thought you liked her underwear anywhere other than on," Rivka parried.

"There is that." Red chuckled, joining Rivka. He used his goggles to take another look at the area. "And if that's all I have to complain about, life is pretty damn good, isn't it?"

"You got that right." Rivka continued around a corner before pulling up. "Got a body."

"Doesn't smell like a corpse," Red offered.

"A Ledonian, not human." Rivka leaned close, covering her face with her shirt collar. "I don't see what killed her."

Red flipped the body with a toe. There was a dried blood stain on her lower chest.

"Stabbed."

"They ran out during the fight, leaving their nice things behind. They never came back," Rivka suggested.

Red continued around the locker room, through the bathroom, and back. "No other doors." He held the door open for the Magistrate. "Do women's locker rooms always look like this?"

"Not as far as you know," Rivka answered. She looked at the strange door with no sign. "Why would they have an entrance like this for the locker room?"

Red shook his head.

"Let's see if there's a men's version." Rivka jogged along the track, examining the wall as she went. The recessed catch was obvious since she knew what she was looking for. She and Red spoke at the same time. "Over here!"

Red pointed to the handle on the opposite side of the gym and Rivka pointed to hers.

"On my way," Red shouted and started running, reaching Rivka in short order. "If I was as fast as Jay, I would have been here before taking my first step."

"That makes no sense." Rivka stepped back to let Red do his thing.

"It makes as much sense as her being able to move like that." Red put his goggles into place and opened the door.

Like the other room, it was dark inside, but the room was different. "This is where the data center used to be."

Rivka hurried inside to find an empty room with computer cables dangling from the ceiling like vines in a rainforest. They had to shove their way through, finding a double door with a ramp beyond that led outside.

"Contact the others. I need to talk to Ankh." Rivka removed her datapad.

How are you guys doing? Red asked.

I was just going to give you a call. We're on the second floor, and you need to get up here sooner rather than later, Lindy replied.

"We have to go right now!" Red yelled out loud.

Rivka was embroiled in her screen, arguing with Ankh.

Red grabbed her shoulder and shook her. "*Right now,* Magistrate. They're in trouble."

Rivka didn't bother shutting the datapad down as she ran after Red, who was done waiting. They put everything they had into sprinting up the stairs, Red weaving from side to side as he climbed. He ran through the building's lobby to the steps and pounded upward with Rivka right on his tail.

"What did they find?" Rivka called.

"I don't know," Red replied.

Rivka didn't bother to follow up. Sometimes it was better to just run.

They reached the second floor in record time, skidding to a stop when they hit the landing. Lindy and Jay were in front of a barricade with angry Ledonian faces staring at them. From an open doorway, more angry faces looked out.

"What do we have here?" Rivka asked holding her hands up in the universal sign for calm as she carefully stepped forward. Red moved to the side, maintaining a clear line of fire at those behind the barricade.

"We have that group," Jay pointed at those behind the barricade, "who want to fight this bunch." She pointed at the doorway before crossing her arms and tapping one foot impatiently. Rivka didn't see any weapons.

"What are you fighting about?" Rivka asked the group behind the barricade.

"They supported the usurper!" the self-appointed spokesman shouted. "Death to them!"

"STOP!" Rivka walked quickly forward, forcing Red to shift position.

"You are supposed to be a civilized society. Act like it!" The Magistrate's words echoed down the hallway. *So this is what it's like when Tod Mackestray doesn't get his payout?*

Shows the value of blackmail, Red replied.

"Don't you know that you've both been manipulated?" Rivka said. She made it sound like a question, but it wasn't. It was a declaration of fact. "Come out here, all of you, and shake hands. You are Ledonians. There is no reason to fight. Fix your problems, and go enjoy this beautiful city of yours."

"Who are you to tell us what to do? Go benji yourself!"

"Benji? Let me start over. I'm Magistrate Rivka Anoa. I'm from the Federation, and am tracking a criminal who may have been the one responsible for the incitement that led to all of this." Rivka waved her hands expansively to take in the entirety of the hallway.

Or the city. She shook her head before continuing, "I

need your help to find the evidence that will clear this up—point to the perpetrators and bring peace back to your planet."

"Dog-snotting long-haired freak!" a Ledonian spat from the doorway.

Red snorted. "You see our dilemma," Lindy explained.

"This fight is over, and you're going to help me get that message out to all of Leed's Planet." Rivka marched to the commenter. The Ledonians were short, their short-furred heads shoulder-high to the Magistrate. She was hesitant to touch one of them, but she had to know. "Tell me what it will take to make peace."

The alien thoughts that flashed through her mind forced her back. She lost her grip and stumbled. Jay caught the Magistrate, having moved to her side at the speed of thought.

"So angry," Rivka whispered. "This was a long time coming, simmering below the surface, and once the catalyst was in place, Leed's Planet came unhinged." She continued in a louder voice, "We need to bring it back together, and that starts right here. Look at what you've accomplished in such a short amount of time. You're destroying your world, just to keep the other guys from getting it. That's insane."

"You don't understand!" the one behind the barricade claimed.

"Help me understand how this is better." Rivka walked slowly toward him. "And don't tell me to benji myself again. You will demonstrate an adult level of decorum. The return to peace starts right here."

"Ha!" The Ledonian made a theatric display of his skepticism.

"Lindy, please bring that one over here, and Red, bring this one."

Lindy closed on the doorway and without a word, grabbed the Ledonian by the back of the head and dragged him into the hallway. Red strolled to the barricade, smiled, nodded, and reached over to grab the rebellious leader by the shirt, dragging him over the top of the barricade.

"Duct tape their wrists together, facing each other. And tape their knees so they can't kick." Jay removed a roll of tape from her small pack, and Red and Lindy made quick work of the Ledonians. They looked like hobbled dance partners until one tried to bite the other's face. The chicken-peck attacks stopped when Red put tape over both their mouths.

"How do we deal with emotional volcanoes?" Rivka asked.

Jay sighed. "We can't. Until such time as they are willing to talk, there's nothing we can do. And yes, this is me, someone who believes a hug will get people through the worst of times. If the rest of them are like these two groups, their entire way of life is doomed," Jay said ominously.

"But for the winners," Rivka intoned in the voice she used when rendering a legal opinion. "The losers shall fear for their lives. Until then, battles will rage like the fires stoked from within. If you can't control your anger, then you deserve what you bring down on your own heads. I cannot judge you more harshly than the crimes you will commit upon each other. That being said, I need to know where the data storage is. It was removed from the basement. Where did they take it?"

Rivka took the taped combatants by the arms and tried to see into their minds. "Where did they take the data storage?" she demanded. Neither one knew. "Dammit!"

She pushed away from them and tried to contact Ankh.

"I might be able to help," a voice said from beyond the barrier.

"Traitor!" someone shouted. There was a scuffle. Jay ran at the barrier and jumped over it in less than a single heartbeat. The scuffle turned into trees felled before a tornado. The Ledonian who had spoken remained standing, while the others were on the floor, groaning in pain.

"Come with me," Jay told him. He tiptoed past the others, unsure of what had happened. Together, they climbed over the barricade. Rivka thanked her with a nod.

"How can you help?"

"I saw the trucks loading."

Rivka intently studied the Ledonian's features but was hard-pressed to see any difference between this one and the others. She thought they looked alike, and couldn't get that impression out of her head. "Do you know where they went?"

"They were government trucks. The government retreated to the main building and erected a massive barricade. I think the data storage equipment would be in there."

"How sure are you?"

The Ledonian shrugged. The group holed up in the room started yelling at him.

"Shut up!" Rivka pointed at them. Lindy grabbed one by

the collar and shook him before tossing him back into the others.

"Zip it," she growled.

"You better come with us," Rivka told him.

"Hello?" a voice said from the datapad.

"Ankh! I've been trying to get you. The equipment was in a side room in the basement, but it's been removed. We think it may be in the main government building."

"That's what I was afraid of," Ankh remarked.

"Since when?" Rivka shot back. "It would have been nice to know that there was some uncertainty in your certainty."

"No matter," Ankh replied. "Go to the main government building and install one of my devices near the equipment. Leave the rest to me."

The Crenellian's face disappeared as the screen went blank.

"Time to go?" Jay asked, wanting to put the anger of the second-floor standoff behind her.

"Thanks for taking care of that. Using your superpower for good." Rivka turned to the Ledonian. "I hope you aren't afraid of running, because I think you'd better come with us. Running is one thing we do a lot of. Maybe you can show us the way."

"It's on the other side of town," he said, brightening with the words. "Thank you. I don't think I could have stayed here."

"Leave them taped together," Rivka said. She pumped her fist and headed toward the stairs. Red waved at Lindy to get in front while he stayed behind to make sure the locals didn't try to follow.

A bottle flew from the doorway and hit Red in the chest. He leveled his railgun, but they weren't intimidated. A second item, a strange piece of metal, flew at him. He easily dodged it, then aimed high and sent a string of hypervelocity darts through the wall above the doorway. When the Ledonians screamed and ran for cover, Red dashed away to join the others.

"You didn't?" Rivka asked him.

"Nah," Red replied. "The little fuckers started throwing shit at me, so I sent them a message, without hurting them. Well, maybe their eardrums are blown, but besides that… They shouldn't have thrown things. Don't bring a rock to a gunfight."

"Usually there's some semblance of common sense, but I didn't see it in either of those two. They were completely embroiled in rage. It was searing," she shared.

When they were outside, Lindy reactivated the mech suit and climbed in. Once upright and combat capable, she started leading the way and then stopped.

Ankh, give me a map, please, Lindy requested.

The map appeared on her HUD and she looked down on the Ledonian, who watched in awe. She activated her external speakers. "I'm taking this road for about three kilometers, turning left and following that road for six kilometers, then turning at a park. Our goal will be on the right. Does that sound correct?"

"That's the long way," the Ledonian replied. "We can take a few side streets, and it'll be a bit shorter."

"We don't care if it's a little longer. We prefer more open space where we can maneuver. Do you know if there are any roadblocks out here?" Rivka asked.

"I don't." He pointed toward the data storage facility. "I was stuck in there."

"Maybe we can hear your story, but for now, we have evidence to collect."

"Our mission, should we choose to accept it, is to break through a military barricade and attack a well-defended position in order to secretly emplace an electronic coin thing," Red droned.

"It's a case, and we're collecting evidence."

"It's a combat mission. All four—five if you count him —" Red tipped his chin toward the Ledonian, "are going to duke it out with the government."

"Maybe they're willing to talk," Rivka suggested, wrinkling her nose at the unpersuasive sound of it.

"Just like those in there." Red didn't need to say the words. It was what they were all thinking.

"Lindy, get hold of Ankh and tell him to fire up the ship in case we need air support."

Roger, Lindy replied over their internal comm before switching to the suit's more robust comm system.

A few seconds later, she gave the thumbs up, hoisted the suit's oversized railgun in one armored hand, and lifted the shield in the other. She started walking at first, and the errant jerking was less than before as the suit continued to compensate. Lindy loped easily along the street, pounding heavily with the mech's armored feet. Rivka and Jay had the Ledonian between them as they supported him. Red filled the position of tail-end Charlie, watching for anyone coming from behind as well as possible ambushes from the sides. Lindy powered forward.

The group ran through ruined roadblocks and the

desolation of a city in distress. The deserted streets echoed with their passing.

We're getting close, Magistrate, Lindy reported.

Slow to a walk, if you would. Let's gather our wits and maybe conduct a fly-by of the building and its defenses, Rivka replied. They looked at Jay.

"With great ability comes great responsibility," Red told her.

She chuckled briefly. "And I was worried that I hadn't been contributing sufficiently to the team." She pointed in the direction they'd been going and the mech nodded, confirming by pointing the railgun.

"I'll be right back." And Jay was gone.

Rivka pulled a water bladder from her small pack and handed it to the Ledonian. He was panting heavily, chest heaving as he tried to draw in more air. He took the water and drank it all. The Magistrate fought against rolling her eyes. Red passed his over, and Rivka took a drink. He downed the rest before checking his railgun, scrubbing at it with a small rag he kept handy for the sole purpose of keeping his weapons clean.

Jay appeared before the group. "He was right. It's a fortress."

"Blazer is ready," Red declared.

Rivka tapped her datapad. "Ankh. We need *Peacekeeper* to open the door for us."

"Because the mission requires air support?" Red raised his eyebrows in challenge.

"Because the case requires evidence," Rivka countered.

"Mission."

"Case."

"I hope that one day I get to live in your world. We're running our asses off and shooting at stuff that shoots back. We're preparing to attack a fortress. That sure sounds like a mission to me, but if you want to maintain your legal fairytale, it's your call."

"You used to have fewer opinions regarding the legal side of my job. I like the new Red. First food bar when we get back on *Peacekeeper* is on me."

"I feel like I missed something."

"Nothing at all. Jay, can you draw us a map of what's up there?"

They squatted around a patch of dirt while Lindy faced away, using the camera in the back of the suit to watch what was going on while still maintaining vigil.

Jay outlined a rectangular building, adding small squares at each corner and then an outer line. "They have a barricade of wire with vehicles with weapons, including tanks. The corner buildings are blockhouses with machinegun-type things on top. There are a lot of people, behind cover, roving and watching. There are also dead bodies out front. It looks like a group approached and the defenders didn't like it."

"They left the bodies?" Rivka wondered aloud.

Red shook his head. "Doesn't sound like they're very happy about all this."

"The anger. Red, would you be so kind as to plan our tactics? I want the evidence, and if Tod Mackestray was the catalyst who turned these people into this, I'll have his head on a platter."

"I think the volcano was ready to blow. A few choice

words wouldn't be enough to send them raging if they weren't already mad."

"Are you arguing to exonerate your old boss?"

Red vigorously shook his head.

"But I agree. Something else was going on here, but once the fuel was lit, we lost the ability to talk to them."

"What's your goal, Magistrate?"

"I want the data but don't want to kill anyone to get it."

Red looked at the diagram drawn in the dirt before taking in his assets. Lindy with the mech suit. Rivka who he was contracted to protect. And Jay.

The Ledonian was restless. "What's up?" Rivka asked.

"I don't live far from here," he answered.

"You can leave anytime you want. You probably don't want to be a part of what's coming. Go on. Once the shooting stops, come on back and see what there is to see."

He nodded and headed out the door.

Red sat back and closed his eyes. "Stay frosty, people. I need to think."

CHAPTER NINE

K'Twillis shambled along with a small contingent of hired muscle. They fanned out to the sides in perpetual flex, barely swinging their arms. Billister walked in front, casually twirling a small pipe. In the small of his back, he carried a blaster in case the pipe wasn't enough.

Since safety wasn't an issue, no fence surrounded the work area. No signs marked the dangerous areas, whether to walk or drive. Great vehicles maneuvered with precision by experienced drivers. Dead and wrecked vehicles were pushed aside. K'Twillis never made a subsequent payment on any of the equipment.

He was always gone by then. He figured the companies would reclaim what was theirs, refurbish it, and put it back into service. Or not. He didn't care either way.

There was a small shack where the mine foreman worked under a false name so he wouldn't be jailed for the shortcuts he was promoting and the resulting injuries.

Only two deaths so far, but those had been buried both figuratively and literally. In the far end of the pit, a hundred tons of tailings, the waste stone after processing, marked their final resting place. No one would dig that up. And those who knew would be eliminated when the operation wrapped up. All the foreman had to do was give the Aborginian their names, and it would be taken care of.

Billister was first into the shack. The foreman jumped but remained in his chair. "You're behind," the security man accused.

"Not by much. We can recover on night shift!" the foreman claimed.

A shadow darkened the doorway but didn't enter the shack. K'Twillis didn't want to get stuck inside the small building.

His microphone helped project his voice. "The original schedule is no longer viable. With the impending turmoil on the council, we have to be finished and gone within two months. You need to pick up the pace. Hire more workers."

"It's not the workers, it's the equipment. We've rented everything that was available."

"Then steal what you need."

The foreman had no idea how to go about doing that. He held up his hands in a gesture of helplessness.

"I thought you were the one who would get things done if the restrictions were removed? We did that, and yet you don't get things done. Are you all talk?"

"No!" the man cried.

"Put your hands on the desk," Billister ordered. The foreman shook his head and started to slide his chair backward. One of Billister's men strolled around the desk and wrapped a thick arm under the foreman's throat and forced one hand onto the desk. Billister raised the pipe, and the foreman screamed.

The pipe slammed into the desk a finger's breadth from the quivering hand.

"Next time, we break every bone in your body," Billister promised.

"I've removed all restrictions," K'Twillis said. "So why are you in here and not out there?" He pointed with a leafy arm.

"On my way," the foreman replied. He tried to stand, but the security man held him in his chair.

"Do you understand how important this is to me?"

"Yes," was all the foreman was able to say.

"Billister and his team of production specialists are going to remain on site until the job is finished." K'Twillis fluttered his leaves in a motion that meant nothing to the humans and humanoids. The Aborginian shuffled away.

The thug holding the foreman lifted him from his chair and threw him over the desk. Papers and rock samples followed him to the floor. He brushed himself off, stood, and apologized profusely as he headed for the door. He stopped and looked at the muscle waiting outside.

Billister grunted. "The last thing you want is for him to return, so what do you say we do a little management by walking around? Let's get the lay of the land and start motivating the good people in the pit to do what he's fucking paying them to do!

"It's a big pit, and there are a fuckload of workers, so I brought some additional efficiency experts with me."

The foreman turned back to Billister. "I know who I climbed into bed with. If those lazy bastards aren't getting it done, they deserve whatever's coming to them—me included. It's a lot of work, but fuck, man, it's good money, and we aren't bothered by regulations or inspectors. Follow me, gentlemen."

"I like your new attitude," Billister stated.

"It's usually not the problem that needs to be solved, but the attitude about the problem. I'm sorry I needed to be reminded of that."

Billister waved for the others to follow them as they stepped onto an angled path along the side of the pit, leading down to where engines droned and whined as they fought against the rock to free the desired ore.

"Margaret, play some violin music," Tod Mackestray told his ship's AI. He continued to lean back and search the media web for opportunities for when his work on Amberstrom came to a close. The news swarm had taken Tip Nel down in a matter of days. Fil Pol was installed as the interim Chairman amid the call for new elections.

The Blokite had no intention of overplaying his hand. He'd earned a cool million and a half from the six-planet conglomerate in the Gridlow Expanse, but it was time to move on. He was looking forward to the next challenge.

"Margaret, how close are we to our target number?"

"Seven million credits," she replied.

"Just a few more gigs and we can wrap things up. Then what will we do, Margaret?"

"Whatever we want, Tod. Fifty million credits is the magic number where you will never have to raise a finger again. You will live in the comfort and style that you deserve."

"I like the way you talk, Margaret. What do you think of the planet called Capstan? There seems to be some turmoil at the highest levels of government, but are they high enough?"

"You have always been surprised at what people will pay to acquire positions of lower power because they see those as leverage to climb higher."

"I used to be surprised by the lust for power, but my entire business is based on it. You are correct that people will pay a half million for a low-level board position, but they want the one seat at the top of the pyramid. All of them. I think I'll raise my prices. Three and a half million to rule the entire planet. When are Capstan's presidential elections?"

"Capstan has a Premier, and the election cycle is already underway. Voting is in two months."

"Perfect, Margaret. That is just perfect. What do you say we leave the good people of Amberstrom to their duly elected and wholly unethical leader while we move on?"

"Capital idea," the AI agreed.

A violin concerto filled the silence while the AI put the *Pandora Express* into the Gate queue.

Lindy wanted to get out of the mech suit. She was starting to sweat. They'd moved inside an abandoned building, where she was half hunched over.

"What do you think, Red?" Rivka asked.

"A diversion late at night; a snatch-and-grab, except it'll be a drop-and-run. Then we wait to see if Ankh can find what you're looking for."

"You want to send Jay in there to place one of Ankh's devices while we have their attention focused elsewhere? That sounds like the plan I was looking for. I don't know why I didn't think of it."

"You feel the anger, don't you?" Jay interjected.

"It's there at the back of my mind." Rivka's face contorted as she confronted the emotions. "I can't believe the power of their feelings."

"Maybe that's the norm for their society?" Red suggested.

"Regardless," Rivka replied, shaking her head. "Two in the morning? Three in the morning?"

"Two. Lindy will light them up on the far corner, destroying the barricade in that area. I'll provide supporting fire. Jay will wait until they start returning fire and then dodge in, get as far inside as she can, and drop a couple of the devices at opposite ends of the building."

"What about me?"

"I can't protect you while this is going on. You stay back and keep yourself from getting hurt. Lindy and I will retrograde in that direction, circle back, and everyone meets up here. The operation should take a grand total of ten minutes."

I only have one question, Lindy asked. *Can I get out of this fucking suit?*

"Yes. I'll handle the first watch, and then the Magistrate will take over so we can get our beauty sleep. Come two in the morning, we get into position and rock and roll."

The mech had already powered down and unzipped the back. Lindy crawled out, stretching when she was free.

"There's a limit to how long one can be in that thing, and I hit it an hour ago." She staggered toward the back of the building to find the bathroom.

"Get some sleep. I'll wake you when it's your watch." Red kneeled behind a front window where he could best see outside. Rivka and Jay found spots to lie down and wait.

Rivka pulled out her datapad and contacted Ankh.

"We will be dropping off your coins tonight. I hope this works."

"If the equipment is operational and if the devices are close enough, I'll be able to gain access to the data," the Crenellian replied.

"That's a lot of ifs." Rivka felt less confident about their chances, but she saw no other plan. She couldn't calm the Ledonians long enough to have any conversation, let alone a meaningful one. "Hold your position, and be ready to provide air cover if we need it."

"*Peacekeeper* is on station at twenty-thousand meters. We can be there in seconds."

"Thanks, Ankh." Her datapad went dark as she signed off.

"No law to research, Magistrate?" Jay asked, laying her hand gently on Rivka's shoulder.

"As much as I want this to be about the law, it isn't. This is about establishing dominance. The one with the biggest stick will be in charge. Quoting the law in the middle of a civil war will get us all killed. Red is right. This is a mission. We'll beat them senseless so we can gather the evidence."

"Don't tell Red that. He'll get a big head."

"His head is already the size of an August watermelon."

The two women chuckled. "I don't know what that is," Jay admitted, "but it sounds funny."

"Get some sleep. This could be over very soon. There's nothing I'd like more than to see Leed's Planet from our tail camera."

Jay held the neutron pulse weapon in her hand. "Take it. I don't want to use it."

Rivka waved it away. "You'll need it more than I will."

"But I won't use it. Once is enough, and I'm glad that I couldn't see what it did to the people inside the tank."

Rivka took the device, turning it over in her hand. It was still dialed to eleven. "We need to stop this war," Rivka whispered.

"Brief me on Capstan, please," Tod Mackestray said pleasantly. He laced his fingers behind his massive head and leaned back.

"Capstan is a minor planet in the Gridlow Expanse, eighty-seven light years from Amberstrom. Population of fifty million, mostly a humanoid race called the Verge, but other non-native species have a presence on the planet, including humans."

"Pause. Did you just say Capstan natives are called virgins?" The Blokite started to laugh. His head remained perfectly still owing to his thick shoulders and lack of a neck.

"'The Verge' is what they are called as a people. An individual member is a Verge."

"You're not making it any better." Tod belly-laughed at his joke. "Pray continue, Margaret."

"Capstan is a pure democracy, majority rules. It makes for a cumbersome and slowly responsive system since any issues that matter are put to a vote. The power vested in the leadership is that they determine what gets voted on. They can bury issues or make them relevant. They shape the message the voters hear."

"That doesn't sound very democratic, but it is perfect for what we do, don't you think?"

"I think you will find fertile ground on Capstan."

"Who is the best target?"

"The challenger, Benitus Fogg, who will lose unless he gets help. He is a wealthy landowner and businessman."

"I like the sound of wealthy."

"He is polling behind because the planet is sound, with a good economy and one of the best educational systems in the galaxy. Status quo suits them. Fogg is running his campaign on a change in focus from liberal arts to business."

"Not everyone gets to be a rich businessman," Mackestray claimed. "Start working up a campaign against the incumbent: shady dealings, personal degradation, a demeaning attitude toward whatever minority group is the most popular, and so on. You know the drill. When will we arrive?"

"To maintain our anonymity, we are routing through

two additional Gates. We will arrive in no more than three days."

"Do they have good food on Capstan?"

"Owing to the diverse nature of those coming from different planets for the education, Capstan has some of the best fine dining experiences in the galaxy."

"That works nicely! Thank you, Margaret. I was going to ask for you to find a planet in between where I could get something good to eat, but I'll wait. Get us to Capstan, and the first order of business, once we arrive, is the best meal on the planet!"

"I will arrange it, along with preparing a meeting schedule for your approval."

The Blokite nodded. He accessed the background information Margaret had compiled and started reading. Leverage consisted of knowledge. He had three days to gain as much of it as possible.

CHAPTER TEN

"It's time to get up." Red shook Rivka until her eyes opened. She sat up and blinked at the glow surrounding Lindy as she climbed into the mech suit. It zipped behind her, and darkness returned.

"I'll go with you," she said as she stood.

"No." Red was firm in his response. "We are a diversion and aren't going to engage. If they try to chase us, we may have to hurt them. Outside of that, it's all Jay on the smash-and-grab."

"What if Jay gets caught?"

"How would that happen?"

"If she stops or someone accidentally opens a door in front of her. I don't know, but *something* could happen. Our luck sucks."

One side of Red's mouth twitched upward. "Aren't we grumpy in the morning?"

"It's the middle of the night." Rivka nodded and slapped Red on the shoulder. "I'll be waiting for you right here. Stay in touch, please!" She tapped the side of her head. She was as guilty as the others when it came to not using the comm chip.

Ankh, can you hear me? she asked.

Loud and clear, the Crenellian responded.

Me, too, Lindy added. Red nodded and gave the thumbs-up before turning his attention back to his railgun. He wore his goggles while he worked.

And me, Jay replied softly.

Right, Red said. *Let's do this.*

Lindy opened the door and crouched, almost having to crawl through. Once outside, she stood up straight and cycled her systems. *I wish the sensors were working. I'm operating on visual only.*

Jay? Red asked.

I'm with you. Let's do this and be done with it.

Rivka crossed her arms, worry lines creasing her face as she watched them go their separate ways, Jay to the right and Lindy and Red to the left, where they would loop around to the far side and attack the security perimeter.

It took the team ten minutes to get into place. No one had to announce the kick-off. That was obvious.

Is that what I think it is? Lindy asked.

Are you talking about the truck that looks to be filled with ammo crates? Nice catch, Red replied.

Lindy targeted it and activated one of her three remaining rockets. It screamed into the night sky, turning at its apex to arrow into the truck. Ledonians nearby started running before the rocket hit, and the spectacular explosion was blinding. While a great cloud billowed from the crater that marked the truck's previous location, Lindy and Red opened up with their railguns, tearing up the pavement in front of the perimeter.

Return fire scattered outward.

Is there an opening? Red asked.

Heading in now. Jay's voice sounded calm, but the comm chip regulated speech, keeping everyone's tone even.

Red and Lindy moved to their first alternate firing positions before renewing their attack to keep the Ledonian defenders pinned down.

After a few seconds of intense fire, Red and Lindy moved to their secondary positions. After their third move, they would fire one last volley and run.

A tank fired, and the round tore through the building too close to Red. A second tank fired, and Red was thrown to the ground. He grunted from the impact of the debris.

Taking them out, Lindy reported. Two rockets launched from her suit.

They have me zeroed somehow. Red covered his head and waited. The explosions following the rockets' impact were his signal to move. *Jay, what's your status?*

Red jumped to his feet and ran to his final position. Lindy's heavy footfalls echoed while he hunkered down and took aim.

The Ledonian rifle fire grew as they gathered their wits and reformed their line, having realized that they weren't the target. Red wondered if they considered him and Lindy to be incompetent.

Status? Red requested again.

They locked me in a room on the ground floor. I don't know if it was intentional, but I stopped to tuck the device under a desk, and the door clicked behind me. I'm stuck.

On my way, Rivka interrupted.

No, Magistrate, stay where you are! Red pleaded.

Overruling you on this one. I need you two to show them who's boss. I've had enough, and if the only way we can stop the madness is by killing them all, then that's what we'll do.

Red switched to a direct channel with Lindy. *She said that, but there's no way she wants us to wipe them out.*

What she meant was clear. Establish dominance. I'm out of rockets, but I'm not out of influence. I'm going to charge their lines. Don't let a rocket surprise me. Or a tank.

She didn't wait for Red to reply before she pounded toward the fortress. Rifle fire increased to a crescendo. Red's gaze darted around the area, looking for any movement to signal the arrival of another tank or an overzealous defender with a rocket launcher. Machine guns burped from the towers.

Red took aim and eliminated the threats. In his mind, he had rationalized that a few had to die so most could live. A small vehicle appeared sporting a variety of antennas.

I think the people in charge have arrived. Stop that small armored car and hold it. Maybe a few hostages will convince the others to lay down their arms.

Lindy slammed into the outer barrier, using the suit's power to toss an overturned car to the side as if it were a toy. She continued like a battering ram, destroying the barricade as she moved until she dodged to the side and sprinted to her target. She grabbed the rear bumper and picked it up, and the rear wheels spun helplessly in the air.

"Put your weapons down!" Lindy blared through the external speakers. She strobed the suit's lights to blind the watchers, and Red saw the opening and ran. Lindy had disrupted their defenses so completely that even if someone noticed his approach, no one fired. He joined Lindy and waved his railgun at the driver.

"Turn it off, put it in Park, and get out." The rear wheels stopped spinning and the engine shut off. Lindy put the vehicle down but maintained her grip. A stately-looking Ledonian climbed from the back seat, and an elder member of the planet's military came from the passenger's seat. The shorter Ledonians looked up at Red while keeping a wary eye on the mech.

"What do you want?" the civilian asked.

"When my boss arrives, I want you to answer her questions."

Lindy made a quick circuit around the perimeter. Not everyone had put down their weapons, but no one dared shoot. Lindy took a rifle from one of the defenders and bent it in half before handing it back. "Be warned." With a clatter, the rest of the weapons hit the ground.

Rivka jogged into the light, slowing to a walk. She nodded at Red and walked up to the one who looked in charge. "Who are you?"

"I'm the president of this world. Which invading terrorist are you?" he demanded with a wave of his arm.

Rivka slowly removed her credentials and shoved them into his face. "I'm Magistrate Rivka Anoa. I represent the Federation. It appears that you are running an unsanctioned war. Every death is on your head, so I'm going to have to take you in for a war crimes hearing." She looked at the military leader. "And probably you, too."

He made the mistake of reaching for her. She was in no mood. Rivka side-stepped, caught his arm, twisted it until the shoulder dislocated, and followed with a right hook that crushed his skull. He was dead before he hit the ground.

"You have been sentenced to death for your attempt to escape custody pending charges of war crimes. You have been judged. Paperwork to follow. Anyone else care to see how quickly Justice can ring across the land?"

The remaining Ledonians stood frozen. The rage at the back of her mind started to ebb. She wrapped her fingers around the Ledonian president's arm, making sure she had a firm grip. "I came here to collect data regarding an individual I wish to question. His name is Tod Mackestray."

Images of the Blokite flashed through the man's mind.

"I see you've used his services."

"I've never met any Tod Mackestray," the president claimed weakly.

"This is going to take too long if you keep lying to me. How about you don't say anything? I'll rip what I want directly from your mind." Rivka stared into his eyes. He tried to look away, but she grabbed his head as she doubled down on her bluff.

"Fine. I double-crossed him, and he did this." The president pointed to the barricade and the soldiers standing around. Red flexed his ham-sized fists. Lindy continued around the perimeter, the rhythmic thumping of the mech's feet keeping the defenders on edge.

"He didn't make you angry. Where did that come from?" Rivka looked over her shoulder. "Go free Jay."

Red nodded and waited. As soon as Lindy arrived, he ran for the front door.

"Things have been on edge for the past couple of years.

We've grown more fractured. I'm trying to bring us back together!" he claimed.

"Remember the part where I told you not to lie to me? I suspect your idea of bringing the people together was simply telling the other side to like whatever you were going to do." Rivka shook her head. "Why did you need Mackestray's help? You weren't going to win the last election, were you?"

"The next election. I had to cancel them once the riots started, and I was forced to declare martial law."

"None of this is your fault, according to you. According to me, *all* of this is your fault. You are guilty as sin." Rivka loomed over the Ledonian. A shot rang out, and the round dinged off the vehicle next to the Magistrate. Lindy opened up with her railgun. Three hypervelocity darts later, only a brown puddle remained where a soldier had stood.

"I'm going to need you to do a few things..." Rivka began, then saw movement out of the corner of her eye—Red and Jay emerging from the building.

I am accessing the Ledonian systems now, Ankh reported.

"I want this to be over as much as you do," the president said smoothly. Rivka backhanded him across the face.

"If you had wanted that, it would have already been done." She let go of him. "Get on the comm or whatever passes for communication on this ass-backward planet and tell everyone the war is over!"

"I can't do that. It'll take a declaration of the council..."

"Are you trying to out-lawyer me with bullshit? I'm the Queen's Barrister, and I have had about enough of you. Your obstructionism in order to continue your illegal war is punishable by death. What are your final words?"

"Wait!" The president dropped to his knees and started crying. Rivka picked him up by the back of his collar and slammed him face-first into the armored vehicle. "Get on the comm and convince everyone that the war is over. Peace talks are underway, so no one is to kill anyone else. You had best lie better to them than you lied to me or I'll remove you and keep going down the line until I find someone who is convincing. How about that?"

The Ledonian opened the door and climbed in. When he tried to shut the door, Rivka blocked it with her body. "I want to hear your dulcet tones sway a world's population."

Damn, Magistrate, you're going to have that crack-snacker begging for buttermilk.

Rivka smiled at the man and motioned for him to do his duty. *Crack-snacker?*

It's better than my original thought, which was scum-sucking asswipe.

The Magistrate continued to smile, trying not to laugh. Jay joined her. "Good job," Rivka whispered, draping her arm over the younger woman's shoulders. "I know how hard that must have been for you."

"I can't kill ever again. You don't know how much that bothered me."

"But I do. I can see the pain you're in. It won't ever go completely away, but it does lessen over time. I won't put you in that position." Rivka stabbed a finger at the president, who had yet to do anything.

"You can't promise that."

"I can promise that I won't do it on purpose. We get into dangerous situations all the time. Your speed will help us resolve things without violence. We almost had what we needed without resorting to full-scale warfare. Almost." Rivka hung her head. When she looked up, she found the president staring at her.

She hesitated for a moment before reaching in and dragging him from the vehicle. She snapped her fingers. "Zip-tie."

Red handed one over, and the Magistrate torqued his arms behind his back until he grunted. She zipped the plastic cuffs tightly.

"Take charge of this thing. I'll be back for him."

"Gladly." Red pushed the Ledonian to the ground and planted a foot in the middle of his back.

"That's one way, I guess." Rivka crooked a finger at the driver. He slowly approached. "Comm. I want to talk to all the government loyalists. In my estimate, that will allow me to talk to exactly half the residents of this planet."

The driver pointed into the vehicle.

Rivka took a deep breath. "Are all Ledonians such flaming assholes?" she asked. The driver shrugged. "Power it up, dial the right frequency or whatever you use here, and hand me the microphone.

"Oh," his mouth formed. He reached through the open door and did as he was told, then handed Rivka a standard microphone connected with a long cord to the unit that occupied the middle of the vehicle.

"All residents of Leed's Planet. I am Magistrate Rivka Anoa from the Federation. I have placed your president under arrest for his perpetuation of an illegal war following his election tampering in order to steal the election. This war is ended, effective immediately. If Federation military forces have to be called in, anyone who is still participating in combat operations will be subject to immediate termination. Leaders on both sides will come to the main government building. This is not a request or a negotiation. This is what you must do if you are to save *your* planet and *your* people."

Rivka repeated herself once before asking the driver to dial the frequency for the other side. He didn't know what it was.

Ankh, what's the frequency for the resistance. The rebels. The anti-government forces, or whatever the hell they call themselves?

There is a significant amount of chatter on one hundred twenty-five point four megahertz. It seems that you've made quite a stir, which also suggests that the main building is under surveillance.

That means credibility that we can do what we say we can, Red remarked.

"One twenty-five point four." She counted on the translation chip to convert it to local units.

The driver dialed it up.

Rivka keyed the microphone and restated what she had told the government forces. "Now we wait."

CHAPTER ELEVEN

"Billister," the man answered the comm. He listened to the voice at the other end. "Yes, sir. I'll take care of it."

K'Twillis' security chief looked from man to man, evaluating who he could trust with removing the members of the licensing board. They had to do it without sending alarm bells screeching across the planet. K'Twillis needed to buy a little more time for the mining operation, that was all.

Billister decided he couldn't trust any of them. "You three." He pointed at a group of thugs looming over a pair of miners fixing a conveyor belt. "Come with me. We have a job to do."

One of the thugs pointed at the men and then his own eyes. "I'm watching you," he growled.

The miners tried to ignore him as they worked to get the belt running.

"Come on!" Billister shouted and stormed off. "Mental midgets," he grumbled to himself.

When they reached the top, a vehicle with darkened windows was waiting. They climbed in and the driver left, not asking for a destination. He had already been told where to take them.

A sketchy warehouse on the outskirts of town, where they had to build a couple of devices before nightfall. That was when the real work would begin.

"How long is it going to take for the leaders to arrive?" Rivka asked, gripping the president's arm to see his answers so he didn't have to speak. Red had put duct tape over his mouth because the Ledonian appeared to be genetically incapable of telling the truth. "They should be here anytime now."

The president struggled against his bonds. Red shook him until he stopped.

"What's the matter? You don't want the people to see you like this? Let me break it to you gently. I'm a Federation Magistrate. You're in my custody because you broke the law. You're not on trial because you've already been judged and found wanting. At this point, you are a convict, but I'm letting you hang around because you have information I need. I'm glad that I can get it from you without having to listen to your perpetual stream of lies. How can you live with yourself?"

"Psychotic?" Jay offered.

That's what I was thinking. Any idea when I can get out of this thing? Lindy asked.

Ankh? Rivka checked in with the Crenellian.

Pandora Express. *The ship went to Amberstrom. From there, it went through a series of Gates with a final destination of Capstan. It should have arrived there within the past day.*

Red's eyes narrowed, and his face turned hard.

"Well then, no time to dawdle," she told the president, who had no idea what she meant. She cupped her hands around her mouth and yelled, "Come on, people! Chop, chop!"

Red couldn't see anyone out there. It was still too early in the morning for light. The president mumbled through the tape.

"What?" Rivka asked, exasperated. She put her hand on the side of his face. "They might attack us? That would be a mistake."

What do you see, Ankh? Rivka requested.

There are vehicles converging on your position. Most are only lightly armed, but there is a heavily armed unit coming down the main corridor in front of you.

If they want to play hardball, finish them.

What is the hardball trigger for action? Ankh wondered.

Rivka stopped for a moment and considered. "Red, we have a military unit coming at us. At what point does *Peacekeeper* turn them into a smoking hole?"

"They might be skeptical of the request. I hate to say it, but if they shoot first?" Red shrugged and walked to Lindy.

"That's what I was thinking." *Ankh, the trigger is if they shoot first. The second that happens, destroy them.*

Lindy moved to a better position across the street to give her a flanking view of the approaching unit.

The first to arrive came from the side streets and drove up to the barricade. Two Ledonians jumped out, using their doors as shields as they took aim. Rivka figured the leader was inside. She strolled into the remnants of the defense. With Red at her side, she crossed her arms and waited.

No one moved.

"Who's here to talk about peace?"

"I am!" the Ledonian shouted from inside the vehicle.

"I'm Magistrate Rivka Anoa. Come out here and talk to me."

"I'm Treacher. How can I trust you?"

"Do you trust the one who claims to be the president?"

"Hell, no!"

Rivka pointed with her chin and Red grabbed the president by the arm, pushed him into an overturned car, and leaned on him, squeezing him between Red's large frame and the vehicle.

"Neither do I, and that's why *I'm* conducting the negotiations."

"How do I know you won't kill me?"

"You'd already be dead," Rivka replied with the old adage. "Come on out, and we'll shake hands. The sooner we start, the sooner this world can get back to normal."

Treacher left the vehicle, ordering his security to stand down before striding purposefully to the Magistrate. He thrust out his hand.

"Are you going to negotiate in good faith?" Rivka asked as she grabbed his hand. Confusion jumped into his mind. Anger boiled, but seeing the president trussed like the criminal he was provided a spark of comfort.

"Of course," the Ledonian replied. "I don't know what normal is for Leed's Planet anymore."

"It'll be a new normal. I can work with you. Thanks for putting your anger aside to do what's right for your people."

A second vehicle raced into the area, then slowly circled. It parked next to the first visitor. No security appeared, just a young Ledonian woman. She made a rude gesture to those waiting in the vehicle before marching straight up to Rivka, dutifully ignoring her counterpart.

"My name is Faith, and I represent the women's faction," she stated confidently.

"Are you going to negotiate in good faith?" Rivka asked, and the two shook.

"I will negotiate on behalf of the repressed. I answer only to them."

Rivka saw the honesty in the female's mind along with unbridled rage. "Since I'm in charge of the negotiations, you will have an equal voice and equal representation."

"I want two votes to make up for the way we've been treated," she demanded.

The first Ledonian rolled his eyes and muttered, "Here we go."

"Shut up, both of you." Rivka took hold of them by their arms and squeezed. "I said equal. I will tolerate no bullshit, quotas, denigration, or demands. You might want to get behind something. The next group brought a lot of their friends."

"I demand..." the woman started. Rivka pulled both contenders behind the nearest vehicle and ducked. A tank round thundered down the street and slammed into one of the guard towers.

The air crackled and tingled as energy weapons came from the sky and painted the invaders, exploding their tools of war. Rivka peeked over the barrier at the nearly complete destruction. A second salvo surprised her, but those were precision strikes to clean up the remainder of the small attacking force.

The enemy is destroyed, Ankh reported.

See if the War Axe *is available for a visit. This planet will self-destruct if we don't hang our biggest hammer over their heads. The only reason they're talking now is because of our firepower and apparent willingness to use it.*

Acknowledged, Ankh replied.

Rivka hoped that the Crenellian would tell her what he had been able to arrange, but she expected she'd find out when everyone else did—after the Bad Company's warship was hovering over the city.

"Who else is coming?" Rivka wondered. "Driver, hand me the microphone, and let's see who else is out there."

She made the call and waited. Only one person answered, and that one had witnessed the destruction of his pro-government unit. "I think you're terrorists, and I will fight you with every fiber of my being."

Rivka turned away from the vehicle. "What is with the fucking anger? You want to see anger? That!" She pointed at the smoking crater and debris where a coherent military unit had been moments before. "You want more of that? I *got* more of that."

I see him, Lindy reported.

Capture him and bring him in, Rivka ordered.

A single round cracked from the mech's oversized rail-gun. Lindy pounded through the destruction and around a corner, and a moment later she reappeared carrying two struggling Ledonians.

She dumped them unceremoniously on the ground in front of the barricade. Red picked them up and carried them to where the others stood. Treacher's lip curled and his fists clenched. Faith crossed her arms and snarled.

"I see you're all friends," Rivka interjected flippantly. "I'm Magistrate Rivka Anoa." She thrust out her hand.

The captured soul started to spit, but Red caught his chin and held his mouth shut as he lifted him by his head. "That's not how you treat a Magistrate," Red growled into the Ledonian's ear. "When I put you down, you're going to play nice, or I will start breaking your bones."

Red let the upstart's feet touch the ground, but he kept trying to lunge. Rivka came close and placed her hand on his arm. She recoiled from the rage. "He's never to see the light of day again. I believe his rational mind is gone." Rivka walked toward the second captive. "What about you? Is there a shred of decency left?'

She grabbed the young Ledonian. More rage, but he was trying to tamp it down. Fear of the unknown gripped him. "I can work with you. What is unknown will become known. What you fear will be exposed and rendered harmless. This is why we negotiate. This is how we achieve a lasting peace. All of you will feel like no one has won, but the end result will be that the people of Leed's Planet will survive and start thriving again."

Red zip-tied the wrists of the angry Ledonian and used

more ties to attach him to the president. "Hey you, do you want to die?" The soldier started to back up.

"No," he replied.

"Then come over here. I have a job for you." Reluctantly, the soldier approached. "Lock these two up. I'll be by later to check on them. If they escape, your life is forfeit. Keep them secure, and we'll *all* walk away from this."

"Let's go inside where we can talk in private. Jay, will you join us please?" Rivka asked. The young woman had been standing to the side and was wearing a long face, but she perked up at being included in helping to shape a better future for a planet tearing itself apart.

Billister had sent the others back to the mine and waited alone in a coffee shop across the street from where the Licensing Board was to convene. He had the impression that they were to meet in the morning but had nothing to confirm that. Billister was prepared to wait as long as it took.

After lunch he took a long walk, always keeping the building in view. He checked in with K'Twillis, who agreed with the course of action. The sun continued through the sky until late afternoon. Billister had his eye on a nearby hotel and was ready to get a room when a series of vehicles showed up, parking out front.

He walked that way briskly, studying the faces to make sure.

The board had arrived. They were consoling each

other, but firm in their commitment to do the people's business.

Billister smiled to himself. *For a few minutes longer, anyway,* he thought.

He strolled casually, turning off the road into a side street where he stopped, fumbled with something in his pocket, adopted a confused expression, and then returned to the corner as if wondering which way to go.

After the last of the members entered the building, he gave them another minute. He took out his comm device, input a number, and held the device to his ear and had a conversation. Any observer would have thought he had called a friend since he interspersed his sentences with laughs and nods. He said a loud goodbye. When the device was in front of him, what would have looked like the tap to hang up was the tap to call the number on the screen.

No one heard the connection as a massive explosion tore through the building. He had been ready for the explosion, but not the level of violence that erupted. It threw him into the air, after which he bounced off a vehicle and rolled into the street. Debris rained down on him and the vehicle. He was barely able to cover his face as he tried to curl up in a ball.

When the immediate danger had passed, the driver got out to help, aghast at the cloud billowing from the rubble that used to be a building.

Billister groaned and tried to get up. The driver told him to stay down.

"No, we have to help. There have to be people hurt worse than me," Billister claimed. When he got to his feet, he felt like nothing was broken, but the bruises would convince others of his innocence. He was a victim of what looked like an accident, like everyone else. "I smelled gas earlier," Billister lied. "I should have called someone or said something! It's all my fault!"

"It's not your fault," the driver said soothingly while he supported Billister. "These old buildings. They ought to do something about them, but it's no one's fault."

CHAPTER TWELVE

Rivka, slack-jawed, looked at the three Ledonians. They were sitting as far away from each other as they could while remaining at the same table. It had been six hours, and they'd gotten almost nowhere. Every point Rivka brought up devolved into angry shouting and accusations.

"The sky is blue," Rivka stated. They glared at each other and then her. "Is there any goddamn thing you can agree on?"

"The sky doesn't matter. We deserve our just slice of it."

"You all deserve what you earn, nothing more, nothing less," Rivka countered.

Faith snarled a harrumph. "If we're kept from earning anything, then we have nothing," she declared.

Rivka wanted to drill down but knew that the anger that embroiled them would not allow them to move forward. They needed time, and to each be given definitive actions to start rebuilding trust. As Federation signatories, they were subject to Federation assistance. Rivka maintained a loose interpretation of that statute.

Rivka didn't know what else to say. Repeating herself was getting them nowhere. She closed her eyes and massaged her temples.

You called? a familiar voice came over her comm chip.

Damn straight, TH, she replied. *Give me a moment with these three, and then I'll bring you up to speed.*

"Here's what's going to happen. The Federation is assuming control of Leed's Planet. The Federation will mandate the actions you will take in order to return to being a functioning member. Your input is no longer solicited. The one thing that you have control over is your people. If any of them does violence upon another, their lives will be forfeit, and you'll be thrown in jail as accomplices."

"You can't do that!" Treacher cried belligerently. Rivka stood and walked to the window. She crooked a finger at them, but they crossed their arms and remained seated.

"Of course I can, and I just did. Any questions? *They'll* be the ones enforcing it." She pointed at a shadow looming over the city.

The *War Axe*—Terry Henry Walton's flagship for his Bad Company. Rivka was pleased to see that he brought company. Dozens of ships formerly of Ten's fleet, which the Bad Company had liberated, followed the destroyer down. As a show of force, the ships were making a slow pass over the city. Rivka smiled at the aerial parade.

She found the Ledonians and Jay standing at her side looking out at the armada.

"Floyd," Jay whispered.

"I look forward to seeing her, too. I'm sure we will, and soon."

Rivka switched to her chip. *Our mech suit needs to be fixed. Good news is that it can take a tank's main round and survive. The bad news is that it hammers the wearer and destroys the sensor suite.*

Sounds like you've had more action than we have. See you soon. Colonel Terry Henry Walton signed off.

"I'll leave you to argue among yourselves, but there's really nothing left to fight over. Because you couldn't negotiate, you'll get to do as you're told instead. That's better, don't you think?"

"No! That's crap," Faith retorted.

"Then you should have come to the table willing to talk instead of wasting your time posturing. I don't have time to babysit. I understand that you have real grievances, but I also see your world in the middle of a civil war. We've been at it for a mere six hours, but none of you have any interest in taking the first steps to resolve this conflict. We'll do that *for* you, and then you can get down to serious negotiations. Here's a tip regarding negotiations: pick the one thing that you must have; that you are willing to die for. That is what you demand. Everything else can be traded or negotiated."

"That's crap!" Faith repeated belligerently.

"That's reality. I didn't come here to stop your war. I came here to stop the person I believe was responsible for starting your war. I now have the information I need to go after him since he's no longer anywhere near here. I'm turning you over to the Bad Company, and they'll prepare you for your Federation oversight team. Now, if you'll excuse me, my friends are arriving, and I want to go say hi."

Jay and Rivka left without looking back. The Ledonians remained in stunned silence.

"There is turmoil in the city," Margaret noted.

"Explain." Tod Mackestray thrived on a certain amount of discord.

"It appears that an explosion has killed every member of the Licensing Board, one of the key committees on this planet."

"How does something like that happen?"

"First reports suggest a gas leak."

"I can work with that, but the sympathy voters will be out in full force. I may not be able to sway things unless a new faction is seeking a way into the system. Any nibbles in that regard?"

"No, but the challengers are stepping into the void, telling the voters that they'll improve infrastructure to keep anything like this from happening again."

Mackestray stroked his chin. He never accepted coincidences during an election cycle. "Who benefits from this board being eliminated?"

Margaret took a while to answer. "The board ensures that businesses comply with regulations to maintain a smoothly operating economy while keeping the Capstan people safe. I can find no evidence of bribery or undue influence of the board members."

"Maybe that was why they had to go. They wouldn't take the money to look the other way."

"I can't find any direct benefit to the current candidates. Anyone waiting for a license would be held up."

"Were there any under review?"

"There were fourteen, in eleven different jurisdictions."

"Someone is trying to horn in on my business. Keep digging. Something is going on there, but I don't expect it'll affect me. Display the profiles of those competing for the top position; those who wish to be the next Premier of Capstan affairs. Come on you, randy bastards, show me what's hidden behind those doors..."

Jay! a tiny feminine voice called. The female wombat called Floyd ran toward her and jumped, but since wombats are not great leapers, she hit the young woman waist high, and both tumbled to the ground.

Lindy clumped across the tarmac and straight into the hangar bay, where she set a record escaping from the suit. Terry Henry and Charumati waved at her, but she was sprinting toward the hatch to the ship's interior.

"Does she know she can go in those things?" Terry asked.

"No doubt, but there's a certain level of dignity we maintain by not fouling the suit."

"Really?" Terry stopped and looked out the open hangar doors, his expression thoughtful. "I've never had a problem."

"You're a man. It's different for us."

"Does it make me a bad man if I've never even wondered about it?"

"It makes you gallingly average in that department." Char shook her finger at him.

Terry bent his knee before her, took her hand, and smiled up at her. "Will you marry me? Please save me from my evil ways."

Char shook her head. "You forgot our anniversary again, didn't you?"

"Was that today?" Terry wondered, searching his eidetic memory for clues. "What day is it?"

"Our anniversary?"

"No, today."

Char pulled Terry to his feet, and the two embraced.

"Are you two still at it?" Rivka asked when she reached the ship.

"One hundred and fifty-some years. One loses track after a while," Terry replied before getting down to business. "You have some issues with the Leed's people, Barrister?"

"We can talk inside. No sense in boring the snot out of everyone else."

A group of Bad Company members approached, aliens and humans alike.

"I don't think you've met our daughter Cordelia Dawn, and of course, Dokken."

Terry covered his mouth and whispered conspiratorially, "She stole my dog."

By all the gods in the universe, the man is completely untrainable. We should keep him in a crate, the dog replied. Cory's eyes glowed blue as she approached, one hand buried in the oversized German Shepherd's fur. With a guarded smile she one-arm-hugged Rivka.

Jay's arms were full of wombat, so Cory settled for a mutual pet of the creature.

"Holy shit!" Red blurted.

Bundin trundled up, surrounded by a human contingent. With his turtle-like shell, four stumpy legs, and blue stalk-like head, he cut an imposing figure. Two humans walked beside him with their hands on his shell.

"Bundin, a Podder from Tissikinnon Four. You know Joseph and Petricia."

When the introductions were complete, Rivka asked if they could go inside and finish their conversation. Terry and Char preferred the outdoors.

"We are stuck on the ship way too much. If there's a chance to be outside, we'll take it." Terry pointed to a short dividing wall between *Peacekeeper* and *War Axe* where they could sit.

Ankh appeared in the doorway of the Magistrate's corvette. Terry and Char waved and yelled, but he only looked at them briefly before continuing his journey. He walked to the destroyer and boarded. He was surrounded by the Podder and others but waved them off on his way to see Ted.

Red hovered near the Magistrate, eyes in constant motion. Leed's Planet was still in a war, despite the pause in violence. Lindy joined him, wrapping an arm around his waist as they watched together.

Char nudged her husband. "I love seeing that," she said softly. He nodded and took her hand in his.

"I do, too. It's a tough universe, but being with the right people makes it all okay."

Rivka looked uncomfortable.

Terry instantly felt bad and redirected. "Leed's Planet. Civil War. No time to negotiate because you're on the trail of a galactic criminal. Is that where we are?"

"We're trailing *two* criminals. One is more elusive than the other, but from the scant evidence we've been able to collect, these two leave a trail of destruction. I can't believe they've been flying under the radar for as long as they have."

"Good that we were on a training mission and could divert here. What do you need us to do?"

"Keep the Ledonians from killing each other until a Federation civil affairs team arrives. They are still armed, but the mech suits are superior to anything they have."

"We'll get the word out. Any hope for them?"

"Yes. They are an emotional people, and I think our guy tipped them over the edge. They are inconsolable right now, but over time they'll earn each other's respect. I hope it doesn't take a generation or two, but it may. The Federation is here for the long term, so this could become a great vacation destination. Who knows?"

"Are any shops open?" Char asked. Cory left the *War Axe* and approached, but stopped and headed toward the corvette.

"There's no one left aboard," Rivka called.

"Look at that little man!" she replied over her shoulder. In the hatch, the white cat with gray spots yowled. When Dokken approached, he hunched his back, turned sideways, and started hissing.

Jay bounced down the destroyer's ramp and put Floyd on the ground. She produced something to throw and tossed it. The wombat ran after it.

"You have quite the zoo going on in there." Rivka knew there was an orange cat on Terry's ship, too.

"What would we be without our friends?"

"Did you actually have Dokken taped to your face?" Rivka asked out of the blue.

"There's a whole story behind that..." Terry started, but Char stopped him.

"I can see you're antsy to get going," Char suggested.

"The thing about the scumbags of the 'verse, they will keep running until you catch them, and then two will pop up in their place."

"We'll take care of things here so you can get going," Terry stated. "And when you're done, we have a favor to ask. We've heard about the slave trading that is riding on the back of the blood trade. We need that to end. If you can find them, we'll do the rest."

"If I find slave traders, I don't think there will be much left for you to do," the Magistrate replied. "I hate those guys. Thanks for everything. I can't pay you for this."

"Training for the Harborians. I don't think we'll be here long," Terry replied.

"Jay! Jay!" came a happy voice. The young woman was carrying the wombat, her face buried in the thick fur.

"I'm not getting my wombat back, am I?" Terry asked the rhetorical question.

"Jay killed some people in my last couple of cases. Those guys needed killing, but that's not who she is. Floyd would be a great help to get the real Jay back."

"I figured. I'll say goodbye. I never seem to be able to keep a pet around."

"There's always Wenceslaus," Char told him.

"He's my arch-nemesis."

"You have an arch-nemesis who lives with you aboard your ship?" Rivka wondered.

"He's not an arch-nemesis. Why did I even say those words?" Char asked herself. "He's the ship's cat. Stowed away."

"Sounds familiar." Rivka nodded.

"You should probably be aware she poops squares that she stacks on top of each other to mark her territory." Char shrugged. "We assigned a cleaning bot to follow her around."

Rivka's face dropped. "Lovely. I don't *have* a cleaning bot." She looked at her security team. "If Red steps in it, he will lose his freaking mind. Probably I will, too."

Cory joined the group as they were saying their goodbyes.

"Dad is a good man," Cory told Rivka. "Selfless to a fault, but you'd better visit often. A wombat, a barrister, and a fellow weapons enthusiast. Your team is filled with the kind of folks he likes to surround himself with. He won't cry over Floyd's absence, but he'll be a bear until he accepts it."

"We can't take Floyd with us. Not in that case."

"Of course you can. She is a gift to us all. How about we ask her?"

Floyd, Terry said. *Do you want to go with Jay?*

Jay! the wombat cried happily.

It means you won't be with us, but we'll visit you when we can.

Terry. I'm sad. But Jay! I'm happy again! the wombat replied.

"Do you mean it? Floyd can come with us?"

"Yes," was all Terry Henry could manage.

A mech clumped through the hangar bay and down the ramp.

"Fixed already?" Lindy asked.

"No. It'll take a while to repair the damage to the other suit, so we swapped yours out with one that's a little bit better."

"What's different?" Lindy wondered, smiling broadly.

"You'll have to see for yourself." The person driving the suit marched straight to *Peacekeeper*. The jets activated, sending it upward, and the mech settled into the ad hoc rack. The back unzipped and Christina climbed out.

"Although I prefer au naturale, sometimes these suits come in handy," she called from atop the corvette. She followed the handholds down. "I'm sorry I didn't say hi earlier, but I was up to my ass in mech alligators. The Harborians are having a hard time adjusting, so we're modifying the suit's software to be more accommodating. I say 'we,' but I mean Ted."

"Of course." Rivka hugged TH, Char, and Cory, and leaned down to give Dokken a kiss.

What are you doing? he asked.

"I was going to kiss you right on your dog nose."

Maybe I don't like human kisses.

Rivka's mouth dropped open, and she looked deeply into his eyes. She found that she could see some of his thoughts. He was hungry for bistok jerky and felt that Terry had some but was holding out.

I'm kidding. I love kisses! He laved Rivka's face with his massive tongue.

The Magistrate fell over backward. "Oh, God!"

Cory pulled her to her feet. "He's incorrigible."

Rivka scrubbed her face with a sleeve. Jay waddled toward the stairs of the corvette, the heavy wombat weighting her down. Hamlet ran when he saw the creature coming toward the hatch.

Red and Lindy waited for the others.

Ankh appeared, carrying a small bag. No one asked what it was, expecting a high tech toy that they wouldn't understand.

Christina waved.

"How's your bar doing?" Rivka asked.

"It's doing too much without me. I should consider retiring so I can manage my business."

Rivka nodded and headed for her ship.

"We brought back the pineapple and ham pizza! It's on the menu now," Terry yelled after her.

The Magistrate stopped. "You did *what*? That's breach of contract. You signed that you would never put pineapple on an All Guns Blazing pie."

"It's this side of the galaxy's equivalent. The contract wording is too narrow, Barrister. It says specifically, 'pineapple.' We've acquired moonsapple, which is identical, and we're using bistok ham. It's wonderful. Stop by Keeg Station and take a walk on the dark side. I think you'll like it."

"No. It's a violation of your contract."

"No, it's not, because we're not putting pineapple on our pizza." Terry shook his head and looked forlorn. "I think I may have to find myself a new Barrister to defend my interests and the soon-to-be-famous-galaxy-wide TH Moonstokle Pie."

Rivka held her head and rubbed her temples. She sighed and tried not to look at the beaming Colonel Terry Henry Walton. "Send me the info on the slave traders. We'll start hunting those scumbags right now."

CHAPTER THIRTEEN

"Chaz, take us out of here. Next stop, Capstan."

The AI lifted off and angled the corvette away from the Harborian fleet that occupied the skies above the spaceport. Once clear, the ship turned upward and raced toward the stars.

"What do we know about this place?" Rivka sat in the captain's chair, surprised when Hamlet appeared. The cat had achieved a truce with the wombat. Floyd didn't care, but Hamlet was not amused by the new addition to the crew.

Jay! Jay! Floyd cried happily over the comm chip into all their minds. Jayita tried to shush the wombat as they played tug. Lindy was still in the shower. Her extended stay in the mech suit had made her nastier than she was willing to tolerate. Red was stuffing his face with a wide array of food bars.

Ankh was in his lab. He hadn't shown anyone what was in the bag he brought from the *War Axe.*

Chaz delivered the standard briefing on Capstan:

demographics, general issues, and key people. He added the latest news, which included the continuing coverage of the complete loss of the licensing board.

Rivka sat up straight, earning herself a claw in the leg. She pushed Hamlet off her lap and started to pace.

"Erasmus, are you around?"

"I am," the AI responded politely.

"What's your take on the licensing board?"

"Capstan is a peaceful society based on working within a loose framework. In many places, lawmaking bodies would do what the licensing board does. They make the regulations regarding trade and oversight. With it, they have a steady and predictable revenue from vendors and service providers. It's also one of the safest planets in the galaxy. Their regulations and oversight create an environment of expectations. Since businesses unequivocally know the framework within which they'll operate, they can better manage their affairs. It works very well for the planet."

"But little excitement, I guess. Police and enforcement aren't present in big numbers?"

"There are very few police and security forces, but regulation enforcement has the largest number of government employees."

"If I read that correctly, the most powerful group of individuals on Capstan died in a single accident."

"That's what all the reports, both public and private, say," Erasmus replied.

"And our boy is there right now as far as you know?"

"*Pandora Express* arrived, entered the atmosphere to

land on the planet, and has not left, as far as orbital control is concerned."

"No ships called *Pandora something* have departed?"

"Orbital control matches departures with arrivals. A foreign vessel like *Pandora Express* would not be able to change names on Capstan."

"Well then..." Rivka stopped pacing. "Red! Can you come in here?"

The big man had been waiting outside the bridge and immediately darkened the hatchway.

"Looks like Tod Mackestray is on Capstan somewhere. Unfortunately, we can't find where he landed his tiny ship. He could have put it just about anywhere."

"We'll be able to find the ship," Erasmus replied confidently. "I'm not concerned about that. Maybe it would be better to flush him out and then use our weaponry to eliminate him?"

Rivka stopped pacing and hung her head. "I can't do that. I know he's done bad things based on the testimony of the people I've talked to, but none of that has risen to capital crime status. I can't execute him without being sure. We have to find him on the ground and arrest him. Then I need to question him, to include questioning his AI to gather more evidence for the case against him. I'll need you for that."

"I look forward to the challenge. My stepfather Plato had to match minds with Ten, the evil AI who was attempting to expand into Federation space using human slaves, the Harborians. Between Plato, Ankh, and Ted, they bested him, destroying him both physically and digitally. It was a glorious victory. I am proud to be one of Plato's stepchildren."

"I want to kick his ass," Red admitted. "That fucker put a price on my head, so I'll be more than happy to secure him for you, Magistrate."

Rivka pursed her lips and puffed out her cheeks. "Just don't kill him. Your word."

"My word, I won't kill him. For your information, Blokites are extremely hard to kill in hand-to-hand combat. They may not be fast or overly strong, but they are genetically predisposed to surviving impacts, probably due to their mountain-dwelling upbringing. They can ram heads with a goat and be okay."

"Good to know." Rivka shrugged since she didn't care about butting heads with goats. She made a mental note to look up what that meant. "Do you have a picture of him we can use?"

Red laughed and shook his head. "I doubt there are any pictures of him or K'Twillis. They are slippery eels, maneuvering through the system anonymously and unobserved."

"Speaking of K'Twillis, any more information on potential whereabouts?"

"None at all. Those two are ghosts until we have the right tidbits. We have to look at the vastness of the sky to find one or two stars that are blocked out because that's where they are hiding. For Tod Mackestray, we were able to narrow where we looked until we found the void in which he hides. For K'Twillis, we are still searching the entirety of an endless universe," Erasmus pontificated.

Rivka winked at Red. "But you are Erasmus, an artificial intelligence like no other. With Ankh, I have no doubt that you will shrink the universe in a way where K'Twillis will stand out like a moon reflecting the sun's light."

"You are too kind, Magistrate," Erasmus replied.

Jay! Floyd cried again. Rivka laughed and shook her head.

"The mood has definitely lightened," the Magistrate said in relief. Hamlet yowled long and low from the bridge. "Except for you, fuzzy kitty."

Jay was tossing a small ball that Floyd ran after, her claws scraping on the hard surface of the deck except where it was rubberized, which was where she picked up speed.

"I love her!" Jay said, her face glowing.

Rivka blinked away a tear. The old Jay was coming back to them. Rivka hadn't noticed how much she had missed the happy-go-lucky teen. She missed seeing Jayita painting on the wall.

"What's next in your mural?" Rivka asked.

"Floyd has to get her place in the picture, so she's next. I think I'll put her right there." Jay pointed to a spot on the wall where each of the Magistrate's team was represented, including Hamlet. "And then the worlds we've seen. I need to capture them."

"'Capturing Capstan.' Sounds like the next hit pop song."

"We need more music," Jay exclaimed. Floyd bounced around with joy before climbing into one of the recliners and falling asleep, snoring within seconds.

"That was interesting," Rivka said.

"Too much excitement," Jay said in a hushed voice, smiling at the wombat as if she were her baby.

Rivka twirled her finger in the air. "We need to talk about our next steps."

"I'll get Lindy," Red said.

"You just want to see her in the shower."

"That doesn't make me a bad person." Red waved Rivka away as he headed for the ship's bathroom.

Ankh, we need to talk about our plan of engagement now that we've arrived at Capstan, Rivka passed using the internal comm chip.

Erasmus is already engaged. Do you still need me? I'm busy.

You are a member of my team, and this is an important meeting. You have to admit that I don't hold many meetings, so when I do, I need you to attend. Rivka waited patiently. She wasn't arguing with Ankh. He was always certain that what he was working on was more important than anything anyone else was doing.

He was usually right.

Fine.

The little victories, Rivka thought. She would have sat down, but Floyd was sleeping in her chair. The other recliner was empty, but humans are creatures of habit. She didn't contemplate sitting in the other, because that was Red's seat. She opted for leaning against the counter that separated the small galley from the rest of *Peacekeeper's* main space.

Ankh appeared right before Red and Lindy, and the three entered together. Red took his recliner and Lindy climbed into his lap. Ankh stood with his thin arms crossed. Jay sat at the table in a chair not far from the sleeping wombat.

"Chaz, show us the general information from Capstan, including customs and things for visitors to be wary of."

The ship's AI ran through a boring series of slides, delivering the narrative in a monotone. Ankh turned to leave.

"That's enough, Chaz. Thanks. Erasmus, show us the information on the upcoming election. Any changes or twists to projections?"

Erasmus ran through the three main races, highlighting that nothing unexpected had happened. The only twist was the accident that killed the remaining members of the licensing board.

"You said 'remaining members of the board.' Did something happen before the accident?"

"Yes," Erasmus replied. "The chairman of the board had an unexpected heart attack and died."

"Timeline for that event, please," Rivka requested.

"Mackestray was still on Leed's Planet at that time."

"He hires people to do the wet work," Red stated, pointing to himself. "He didn't need to be here."

"But what does he get from nuking the board? They may run the show on Capstan, but trying to influence that many at one time seems odd."

"I don't know. He destroyed people without killing them." Red scowled and looked at the deck.

"I think we're missing something," Jay offered.

"I don't see any causal links. I believe Jayita is right. We're missing something. I shall re-evaluate all the data," Erasmus said.

"Where's that leave us, Magistrate?" Lindy asked.

"Without a lead. You know what we do when we don't have any leads?"

"We scare some up!" Jay declared.

"Let's meet with the three challengers first. They have the most to gain from Mackestray's influence."

"They have the most to lose, too, once they join the Blokite's brothel." Red sneered.

"A vote for Bandersnatch is a vote for progress!" The message blared from massive speakers hanging on the front of the building.

"No laughing," Rivka warned the others before leaning through the cab's window and talking to the driver. "If you would wait, please, we won't be long."

"Meter's running," he replied, smiling and kicking back with his hands behind his head.

"As I would expect." She followed Red as he hurried through the front doors to get away from the noise. Jay rushed in after him with her hands over her ears. Rivka and Lindy were slower. "Don't stay out here. I don't need you to be driven insane."

"I don't want to go mad, so that works for me. I'll wait inside the front door. I hope they aren't grinding eardrums the same way indoors."

Rivka winced. "Only one way to find out."

The heavy doors and windows protected them. They both breathed a sigh of relief, taking deep breaths as if the air were fresher.

Rivka strolled up to someone who looked important.

"I'm the Magistrate and I need to see the candidate, please. I believe I have an appointment."

"I'm afraid not," the female said. "Because he's not here. He has a rally on the other side of the planet."

Rivka pulled out her datapad and tapped to the confirmation message from the candidate's office. She showed it.

"There must have been some kind of mistake. That communication doesn't change the fact that he's not here," the Capstanian replied. Nearly indistinguishable from a human except for the lack of ears, the female stood her ground.

"No problem at all," Rivka smiled and extended her hand. When the female took it, Rivka followed up. "Are you sure he's not here?"

In her mind was a picture of him in his office and her wondering if he'd been seen.

Using her nano-modified strength, Rivka started to squeeze the woman's hand. "Why are you lying to me?"

"You're hurting me!" the Capstanian cried, trying to free herself. She was beginning to panic, and her mind became a jumble of thoughts from which Rivka could see nothing substantial.

The Magistrate let go. "We'll be going in the back now and meeting with the candidate. Lindy, hold her."

Lindy towered over the Capstanian, grabbing her collar and lifting until she was standing on her tiptoes.

"You can let her loose once we are in the company of Bandersnatch. He doesn't have a woman back there, does he?" Rivka asked, remembering the unpleasant scene with the Reman mayor. "We won't be long."

CHAPTER FOURTEEN

K'Twillis looked into the pit, remaining close to the foliage, away from the edge. His leafy non-sentient brethren made him feel at home, while the torn world before him reminded him that he didn't care about the planet. It was something to be exploited.

Nothing more.

If the people departed, the flora would reclaim the land and save it from itself. Maybe the residents of Capstan would leave this part of their world, but they probably wouldn't. K'Twillis would be long gone by then, riding with the prize of a full freighter of exotics, the sunlights of a hydroponic section keeping him fed and spry.

The freighter was half-full already. They were getting close.

"My compliments, Billister," the Aborginian said through his strange microphone. "Production is back on track."

"Just doing my job, sir." Billister stood apart from his boss. He refused to get too close, because he had enemies, too. It wouldn't do for an irate husband to harm the Aborginian while shooting at the security chief.

"It's more than that. Masterful work with the board. They never discovered that it wasn't an accident."

"It *was* an accident. They were on a train headed down the wrong tracks by trying to cross you. It didn't turn out well for them."

"I like when my team is better than their team—which is always, because I like to win."

"Losers think winners are lucky," Billister remarked. "Winners make their own luck."

"Winners are playing to win." K'Twillis shifted to get more sun while remaining close to a bush and a tree. "I like you, Billister. This is the third planet we've been on together. You get things done. The rest of that rabble will remain here when we move on. They have come up short of my expectations."

"I couldn't agree more. With more time up front, I can hire better people who require less training." Billister waited, but K'Twillis didn't respond. "That was not meant as a criticism, sir," he apologized. "I offer it as an option for a future project. A little more time and a lot less hassle."

"I had very little hassle." The microphone failed to translate emotion, but Billister suspected the Aborginian had taken it the wrong way.

"My apologies. I shall carry out your will in whatever time I am given."

K'Twillis' leafy body shook as if he were laughing. He didn't raise the microphone to articulate his position.

"I see eight days remaining. Then we leave."

"The foreman is planning for fourteen more days of work."

"Exactly," K'Twillis replied cryptically. "Tell no one."

Rivka knocked politely and then tried to open the door. It was locked, so she nodded to Red. He took one step and slammed into it with a huge shoulder. The door burst open. Bandersnatch sat behind a desk, buried in papers and tablets.

"What is the meaning of this?" he demanded before taking a good look at the group that had forced their way into his office. He didn't recognize the logo on the collar of Rivka's Magistrate jacket, but he knew the power of railguns.

"I'm Magistrate Rivka Anoa, and we had an appointment that your lackey tried to chase me away from. That tells me you've got something to hide. As Premier for Capstan, you would be your planet's representative to the Federation. Is this how you intend to treat us?"

"Today was always a down day in the office. If I had made an appointment, I would have kept it, but I don't see anything on my schedule." He leaned forward as if making a profound point to an awed nation.

"Most politicians are smooth liars." Rivka strolled around his desk to get within arm's reach. "Tell me, have you heard of an individual named Tod Mackestray?" She patted the back of his hand in a friendly manner. Images strobed into her mind.

"I don't know anyone by that name. It doesn't sound

Capstanian. Is she an alien?" From what Rivka could tell from the snippets of thought, Bandersnatch was telling the truth.

"*He's* a Blokite. Impossible to miss. Sells influence. I thought you might be a prime customer."

"I have a good chance to win!" he claimed.

Rivka raised her eyebrows as she sat on his desk and looked down on him.

"It's a slim chance," he conceded.

"How far behind are you in the polls?"

"Seven percent. No one has ever come back from a margin greater than five this close to the election." He threw his hands up in frustration before pointing at his desk. "There's nothing here that will help me get over that last hurdle. I know I can do a better job for the people, but I just can't convince them."

Rivka touched his arm. He believed what he was saying. She wondered if he was psychotic. Selfless service in government. She bit her lip to keep from snorting.

"I appreciate your time, Mister Bandersnatch. Ping me if you hear from Tod Mackestray. He's an intergalactic criminal. He's here on Capstan, and I aim to catch him." She turned toward the door. "Red, get the cab and bring it up front."

The taxi with the Blokite had to wait for another cab to finish loading. He was taken by a trio of striking women climbing in. The last sported military clothing and carried a railgun. He liked everything he saw and was in need of a new chief of security. He made to get out, but the door was locked.

"Need to pay first," the driver said, smacking his lips.

"Wait for me. I'll need a ride when I finish. Let me out!" Mackestray kept pulling at the handle, but it wouldn't give. He groaned as the woman closed the door behind her. The cab raced into traffic and disappeared. "Now look what you've done."

Mackestray tapped his credit chip against the payment device.

"You want me to wait?"

"That was what I said." The Blokite glared.

"Two hours pre-paid, then. Tap the chip again."

After the new charge registered, the driver put the vehicle in park. "I'll be here when you come out."

The door unlocked and Mackestray was finally able to open it and escape. He stood on his tiptoes but couldn't see where the other cab had gone. He slammed the door and headed through the noise of blaring megaphones. "How do these people live like this?" he grumbled.

Inside, he found a severe-looking Capstanian female. She smiled and nodded when she saw him. "He's in the back," she told him.

He walked by with barely a glance to acknowledge her.

When he reached the office, he stopped to take in the broken door. He slowly pushed it open, wondering if he'd find a dead body inside. Bandersnatch was behind his desk. He turned pale when the Blokite entered. Mackestray shut the door as best he could before taking a seat on the couch against the wall.

"I hear you're down seven points. If you want to win, I can show you how."

"Who. Are. You?" the candidate asked slowly, knowing full well who was in his office. He found his mouth dry. Railguns appeared before his eyes, and a Federation Magistrate glaring at him. He started to sweat.

"I'm Tod Mackestray, and before the day is out, we're going to be good friends."

"Next stop, the incumbent," Rivka told the group. "Let's see if he is willing to meet with us. I don't want to break down any more doors."

Jay watched out the window.

"I don't understand the licensing board," Rivka said slowly.

Jay shook her head. "I understand why people want to be in power. There's nothing selfless about it. My parents taught me all I need to know about bureaucracy."

"I would like to think that your parents are outliers, but I know that isn't true. I have hope that there are some good people out there. I didn't see anything bad from Bandersnatch."

Red covered his mouth as he chuckled.

Rivka shook a finger at him. "Maybe this planet is too mellow for someone like Mackestray to find traction."

Red straightened up. "If that's the case, we need to hurry. If he leaves, we'll be back to square one."

The Magistrate considered Red's point and took out her datapad. "Ankh, we need to make sure that *Pandora* does not leave Capstan space. Can you file an alert through Federation channels, please?"

"Yes," the Crenellian replied. "Jay is not allowed to leave the ship without Floyd."

"What makes you say that?" Rivka asked.

"What's wrong with Floyd?" Jay demanded, suddenly alarmed.

Ankh rotated the camera to show the wombat sitting on his lap, nuzzling him with her broad snout. Since Floyd was nearly the same size as the Crenellian, the wombat filled the screen.

"I'm glad you two are getting along," Jay said, relieved.

Ankh didn't look pleased. His usual neutral expression had been replaced by one of disdain.

"You need to get back to the ship as quickly as possible. Five minutes ago would be best."

Rivka shook her head. "No can do, Ankh. We have one more stop, and then we'll return to the ship. I'm sure Floyd would like to see the city. She'll be a big hit, since I haven't spotted any domestic creatures." Rivka watched the sidewalks and the nearby traffic, seeing no animals of any kind.

Ankh's face disappeared as the wombat started jumping up and down in front of the camera.

"Sorry, Ankh. Gotta go. Remember to file the alert on *Pandora Express*." Rivka tapped off before Ankh could demand they save him from a happy wombat.

"Premier Bumperclasp." Rivka cleared her throat after

saying the name. Red steeled his expression. "I'm glad you were able to meet with me."

Rivka offered her hand, and as he took it, she said in a rush, "Do you know a Tod Mackestray?"

His mind reflected nothing in regard to the name. His words were true. "I don't know that person."

"A Blokite," Rivka replied. "He's in the business of election tampering, and we've followed him to Capstan. He is here. What's he doing here? That is the question I'd like an answer to. Regardless, he's an intergalactic person of interest. I need to talk to him. If you see him, please detain him and contact me. We'll come to collect him."

"Is he dangerous?"

"Judging by what we saw on the last planet he visited, yes. He might be responsible for thousands of deaths."

The premier sat down heavily and blew out a long breath. His brow furrowed. "And you say he's on Capstan?"

"Yes, but he's slippery. If you send your people after him, I fear that he'll run and we'll lose him. With your elections pending, he'll be soliciting clients. We want him to stay in the open. We've issued an alert for his spaceship through the Federation, but that won't mean much if he runs. I don't want him to escape. The damage he's accused of doing is rather significant."

"It doesn't sound like you know for sure he's the one you're looking for."

"We know he's committed a number of crimes. But has he committed the worst of the crimes? It's my job to find proof of that. I'll be able to tell by questioning him."

"What if he doesn't talk?" The premier wasn't convinced.

"He doesn't need to. I'll know," Rivka replied.

Bumperclasp nodded and offered nothing else.

"The issue of the licensing board has come to our attention. It seems out of character for Mackestray to do something like that, but I don't believe in coincidences."

"Our investigators found no evidence that it was anything other than an accident. Although nothing like this has ever happened before, it's not outside the realm of possibility. It was a tragic intersection of bad luck."

"What about the chairman of the board's death?"

"That happened the week before. A heart attack. Once again, it's not common, but not unheard of. They are coincidences, nothing more."

Rivka chewed on the inside of her lip and studied the premier as he spoke. "I'd like to look into it as part of my investigation into Mister Mackestray." She wasn't asking permission. "Who do I need to talk with to find issues that were on the board's plate in order to eliminate concerns in various lines of inquiry?"

"The secretariat that supports the board. They are currently in mourning. The recording and documentation office worked closely with all the board members. They were friends. I'm not sure how much you'll be able to get from them. Please take care, Magistrate."

"We will be empathetic. No one likes to lose a friend." Rivka had nothing else. "Thank you for your time. If Mackestray shows up, please let me know. And I have one more request. We need the assistance of your law enforcement personnel."

"My people out front will put you in touch. You have my full support. I don't like the idea of someone who may have been responsible for thousands of deaths roaming free on my planet."

"Thank you." Rivka was sincere in her appreciation even though the words were simple.

The premier nodded and returned to his work. Rivka and her team showed themselves out, leaving their contact information with the premier's team of assistants. A Capstan federal authority van was ordered and arrived within minutes.

I would have thought they'd be busier, Red said privately.

They are convinced it was an accident. I'm convinced of the opposite, Rivka replied.

"Back to the ship to collect Floyd, and then to the recording and documentation office," Rivka said aloud.

"Floyd will be fine," Red suggested. He fidgeted impatiently.

"It's not Floyd we're worried about. It's Ankh. The little guy could be smothered to death, and then who would change the lights to green for you?" Lindy asked.

"We're not going to let Mackestray get away," Rivka tried to reassure him.

It wasn't very reassuring. They were grasping at straws.

CHAPTER FIFTEEN

Jay hurried into *Peacekeeper*, calling for Floyd. The wombat bounced down the corridor to meet her, and Jay quickly kneeled to avoid getting bowled over. The two hugged before Jay carried her friend from the ship and rejoined the others waiting in the van.

"Hey, Floyd!" Rivka smiled. "How was Ankh?" she asked Jay.

"Never saw him."

Ankh! Floyd cheered in her small voice.

"He's fine," Red grumbled before directing the driver to head out.

"The Chief Constable wants a word," the driver said.

"I look forward to it." Rivka had grown comfortable with her authority and wasn't intimidated by local law enforcement. She needed something, and he could provide it. She would get what she wanted, and in the end, the galaxy would be a safer place.

The van raced through the city, using its lights and

siren to bypass normal traffic. "The roads can be bad this time of day," the driver said to no one in particular.

"I lived on a massive space station," Jay whispered. "How come most of the planets we go to aren't advanced? Collum Gate had hover vehicles and cool architecture, but most places are backward."

"Because most places are playing catch-up. Without the Federation, many of these races would still be stuck on their own planets. The Federation helps them technologically, but only incrementally so their social systems can keep pace. That's why it seems like so many of them are stuck in a twentieth-century Earth kind of place. The Federation expanded so quickly that they introduced advances at relatively the same time."

"So here we are, stuck in the same traffic on different planets. I wondered why that was, but your explanation makes sense." Lindy continued to look out the window as the world of Capstan raced by.

The law enforcement center was in a nondescript building in an average section of town. There were no high rises. There was a small compound where official vehicles were stored. The entrance was a simple double door with a small logo and the name of the organization.

Capstan Federal Authority.

Red hopped out first and prepared to go inside, but Rivka stopped him. "I assume that your railgun will be less than popular until we establish our bona fides. You and all your hardware wait in the van. I'll call if there is an issue."

Jay climbed out with Floyd who immediately ran to the bushes and dropped a load.

Rivka groaned as she looked at Jay, who held up her hands. "No bags. Sorry."

Feel better, Floyd claimed.

"I'm not sure she should come inside."

"You're not going alone," Jay told the Magistrate, putting her hands on her hips. "And we're kind of a matched set." She pointed with her chin toward the wombat who was sniffing her way to the front door.

"Sounds good," Rivka replied, shaking her head and walking toward the door. Jay hurried ahead and pulled the door open. Floyd squeaked through right before the Magistrate.

Hold up, little girl, Rivka said. *Wait for Jay, and you two stay together, please.*

But people! Floyd complained.

You'll get to meet them, but I need to introduce you, Jay remarked.

Floyd ran back to meet Jay at the door. When Rivka looked up, she found every Capstanian in the front lobby staring at them. Rivka smiled and waved before holding up her credentials. "I'm Magistrate Rivka Anoa, and I have an appointment with the Chief Constable."

She looked for someone to acknowledge her, growing more and more irritated at the increasing length of the delay. A uniformed officer looked around before stepping forward.

"I'm Officer Dellagrouch. I'll escort you to the Chief Constable's office."

"Thank you, Officer." Rivka's smile returned. The officer pointed at the wombat and started to speak, but

Rivka stopped him. "Her name is Floyd, and she's coming with us."

The officer seemed to instinctively know that point wasn't to be argued.

"Shall we?" Rivka motioned into the building. She had no idea where the Chief Constable's office was and was glad of the escort.

Rivka fell in beside the officer, making small talk as they walked. Jay and Floyd followed, the wombat bouncing happily and nodding at the people as she passed. A couple of braver souls kneeled to say hi and were warmly greeted with a full body rub of Floyd's soft fur. She radiated happiness, so it didn't take long before the entire station was following in order to feel her fur and greet her.

"Here we are," Officer Dellagrouch said, pointing the way through an open door. The Chief Constable, an ancient Capstanian, walked slowly toward the door with his hand outstretched. Rivka shook the warm hand. There were no ill thoughts, and Rivka relaxed. The Chief Constable looked at the wombat.

"We don't have pets on Capstan, but off-world entertainment often shows them. I always wondered what it would be like."

"Her name is Floyd, and she's a wombat," Jay informed him.

"Nice to meet you." He leaned down and held out his hand. Floyd nuzzled him, rubbing her head against his hand. He stroked her fur and smiled.

"Floyd is a member of our crew. She is free to do as she wishes, but we take care of her."

The wombat stood on her back legs, and the Chief

Constable caught her against the front of his trousers. He scrubbed the fur on the side of her neck, and she vibrated in delight.

"I think we've been missing something. I shall have to explore this in my retirement. Constable Crustcrumb's Companions. It has a certain ring to it."

Jay helped Floyd down so the Chief Constable and the Magistrate could have their conversation.

Crustcrumb's clothes were covered in wombat hair. He looked at his hands as if the Black Plague had infected his office. "Oh my," he exclaimed.

"That is the one drawback of pets or hairy companions." Rivka took a seat in one of two chairs before his desk. "You said you wanted to talk to me."

He tried to wipe off the hair, but it stuck everywhere. Soon, it was on every surface of his clothing. He finally gave up. "I wondered how I could assist with your investigation, Magistrate."

"I would love your help. We're looking for a spaceship called *Pandora Express*. It's a small yacht. It could have landed anywhere. We already tried the usual search and came up with nothing. I think you probably have access to resources we don't." Rivka flashed him a smile.

"Yes. We have the eyes and ears of our people, which are more valuable than any of those computers. I can put out an all-points bulletin."

"There's the rub. He can't know that we're here and looking for him. We believe he has an AI who taps local communications and data systems to gather information that he then uses to blackmail people. He's used blackmail and hacking to influence elections. That is where he gets his kicks and his credits."

"That changes things. We can brief it verbally for the crews, but we can't hit the day shift until tomorrow morning. They are already on patrol."

"As long as we tread softly, another day is perfectly fine. Tod Mackestray is his name, and he's a Blokite."

"I don't know that species," the Chief Constable admitted.

"They evolved to survive impacts to their head, neck, and back. They look like a humanoid battering ram." Rivka accessed her datapad and pulled up an image.

"Is that him?" the Chief Constable asked.

"No. That's a picture of the Blokite ambassador on Collum Gate."

"They look fairly intimidating," he suggested.

"You don't want to fight one hand to hand. It's almost impossible to hurt them."

"Motive, means, and opportunity, Magistrate. Motive is money. Means is via his AI and personal intimidation. Does he have a gang that works for him? And opportunity. He's here, and can get on any communications device to call. His personal appearance is probably the easiest for us to find, but we fight hard not to be accused of racism. I suspect there aren't many Blokites in the universe, but even so, we can't stop one for being of that race. We need some other reason to check his identification."

"I'm sorry, but I don't have a picture or something confirming that he's the one who came from *Pandora Express*. I still believe you have probable cause to stop every

Blokite and at least ask for identification. If nothing else, simply tell me, and I'll take care of it."

"I can't do that, Magistrate. We pride ourselves on freedom and equality."

"I respect that, but when you have a fifty percent or better chance that someone is who we're looking for, I'm good that we haven't violated anyone's rights. I'd take a twenty percent chance. I can't believe there are five Blokites on Capstan."

"Maybe *you* can take that chance, but I can't and won't. I am sorry, Magistrate."

"Don't be sorry, Chief Constable. I can respect someone who stands firm to their principles. A couple other tidbits came to me while we were talking. He has an AI called Margaret whom he talks to, and he'll probably visit candidates for office or politicians who are already in office. Maybe if a Blokite shows up in those ways, it'll meet your threshold for intervention."

"In either of those cases, yes. There is no reason for a Blokite to be interested in our elections."

"Deal, Chief Constable. If you find *Pandora Express*, please let me know. We'll lock it up so he can't fly out of here and then we'll tighten the noose. If you can't tell, I want this guy in a bad way."

"Stay true to your principles, Magistrate," the old Capstanian advised. He wasn't trying to be sarcastic. He'd been in the business a long time and knew the slippery slope of taking shortcuts.

"I will. There are those who would kill him on sight. I'm not one of them. I want to question him. I already have a substantial case built, but I need a few more answers to finalize the case."

"As a Magistrate, is it true that you are the judge, the jury, and the executioner?"

Rivka studied his expression, wondering what answer he was looking for. She settled on the innocuous.

"I mete out Justice to the guilty. Magistrates carry the burden of the Federation. We deal with the worst of the worst. I've been shot, shot *at*, blown up, jailed, boiled, and watched my people get hurt, all of that over the course of eight months. I have little tolerance for games. When the end comes, there is no hesitation."

"I am happy to not have your job, Magistrate."

"I am surrounded by good people like Jay and Floyd. My bodyguards are outside. I didn't think you'd appreciate two folks carrying railguns inside your station."

"That was probably the right call, but we would have been okay. You are a Federation Magistrate. We will get the word out regarding *Pandora Express* and have our people continue their search on the down low. We'll make sure they don't broadcast the search. Good luck."

"We'll take all the luck we can get. Like I said, this guy is slippery. And we're also looking for an Aborginian named K'Twillis."

"An Aborginian. A swamp person, if I'm not mistaken."

"That's right." Rivka's ears perked up.

"I think there's one here. Interesting that such a being is invested in mining, but there it is."

"Mining!" Rivka ripped her datapad from inside her coat and started tapping. *There's an Aborginian here who is interested in mining.*

That's him, Red declared. *They are both here? Holy. Shit. Lock and load, people. The hunters become the hunted.*

Ankh. Check if the licensing board was doing anything with mining permits preceding the chairman's death. It seems that K'Twillis may be on Capstan as well. Search everything to do with new mines, rented mining equipment, and so on.

"You have been an incredible help, Chief Constable, but I need to go. We have the scent, and can't let it go cold." She tapped the side of her nose, then raced from the office with Jay and Floyd running after her.

Fire up the van. We're on our way. First stop, the recording and documentation office. We need directions to the mine. We have an Aborginian to find.

Don't forget Tod Mackestray, Lindy said.

They have us surrounded, so no matter which direction we shoot, we're going to hit something! Red declared.

The Magistrate burst out the front door, running for the van. She jumped in and turned to find Floyd heading for the bushes with Jay jogging after her. She relieved herself, and Jay carried her the rest of the way to the van.

Tired, the wombat cried. Rivka helped them into the van before Red told the driver where they needed to go.

"Does this count as running?" Lindy asked.

"I thought Ankh won the pool?"

"He did, but there's a new pool. It resets with each new mission…I mean case," Lindy explained.

"It does *not* count as running," Red stated definitively. "But we may be shooting pretty soon. I think my number might be up."

"We could take that a couple different ways," Rivka

interrupted. "Dammit! Why do we always devolve into those damn prop bets of yours?"

"Combat, Magistrate." Red held Rivka's gaze. "It's the most inappropriate place for the best humor. Roll with it."

"Nobody gets killed!" she insisted.

"We'll do our best," Lindy replied.

Floyd started to whimper and stuffed her snout under Jay's arm. "Nobody says the 'd' word. Floyd suffered enough of that when the Bad Company rescued her. She's been safe ever since."

"Joining *us* to be safe?" Red mumbled.

Rivka stabbed a finger into his exposed flesh and made the zip-it motion across her lips. Red nodded his apology. The Magistrate shook her head.

CHAPTER SIXTEEN

The datapad vibrated. Rivka looked at it and scowled. "Mackestray showed up at Bandersnatch's right after we left. He's already gone, and the candidate doesn't know where."

Red hammered a fist into the dash, much to the driver's chagrin.

"We can't be in two places at once," he growled.

"We don't have to be." Rivka used her pad to call the Chief Constable. The person who answered patched her through. "Mackestray visited Bandersnatch. Is there any way you can put a watch on the candidate's office?"

"I work for the Premier. Bandersnatch is running against him. Do you know how that would look? Even if I tried using someone in plain clothes, it wouldn't work. I'm sorry, but I can't do it."

Rivka's lip curled, and she clenched her jaw as her fury rose. She fought to keep it in check.

"I understand. Just stay out of my way." She signed off before he could respond. "Looks like it's just us and our dilemma of having to be in two places at once. I'd call the Bad Company to help us out, lock down the whole planet until we caught these two, but we left them in the middle of a shit sandwich. We're on our own."

"I'll watch the candidate's office," Lindy volunteered.

"Mackestray is dangerous," Red argued slowly, knowing there were few options, none of them savory.

"So am I," Lindy replied.

"He could have a bodyguard, someone like me."

"I'll be okay. I'll call if it looks like more than I can handle."

"What would it take for you to call?"

"Maybe a dozen. Ten tops, if they were big." Lindy smiled. Red had no comeback.

"We could go with her," Jay offered.

Tired, a small voice said.

Rivka put a gentle hand on the young woman's shoulder. "Floyd is an absolute delight, but she is comparable to a four-year-old, maybe?" Jay nodded. "You need to keep her out of harm's way. You two go back to the ship. Lindy, set up camp at the office. Red and I will continue to the recording and documentation office."

"Driver, can you get them a ride?" Red asked.

Without answering, he accessed a digital radio. In a few moments, he pointed. A patrol car waited for them up ahead. Before the van stopped, Rivka had the door open. Jay still carried the wombat, while Lindy was fully armed. They made an eclectic pair on the sidewalk.

"We want him alive," Rivka reiterated.

"Good luck," Jay replied as the Magistrate shut the door and the van rolled away. Out the back window, Rivka saw the doors pop open on the patrol car and her people climb in. "Fate has smiled on us, Red. Let's not dick this up. Fate makes second chances costly."

Red's knuckles were white from how tightly he gripped his railgun.

The driver made short work of the route to the office building. Red led the way inside with Rivka close behind. Once out of the open she looked for a person to talk to, seeing a sign for the manager aside a corner office. Someone tried to stop them, but the Magistrate waved them away.

She knocked on the doorframe before entering the office. Besides the female Capstanian behind the desk, a visitor occupied the sole chair in front.

"I'm sorry, we'll be a little while. You'll have to wait outside," the manager said.

"I can't wait." Rivka showed her credentials. Red stepped close enough to get the visitor's attention and pointed toward the door.

"Please wait outside. We won't be long." The tone of his voice suggested that it wasn't a negotiation or conversation, or anything other than a direct order. She didn't bother to argue, rising and leaving the office. Red closed the door behind her.

"An Aborginian is in charge of a mining operation. We need to know the details."

The manager accessed the files on her computer. "Permits have been applied for and preliminary work done, but I can assure you, there is no mining ongoing. Name on the permit is for an Aborginian company called Key To Will Is Life."

"K'Twillis." Rivka leaned forward. "I can assure you that mining is ongoing. I am seeking this individual as part of the intergalactic illegal exotic minerals trade. The Aborginian is to be held for questioning."

The manager pressed Print. "Here are the addresses for the mine, the business, the safety officer, and the equipment rental company."

Rivka used her datapad to send the information to Ankh. It only took him seconds to reply.

The business address is fake. The imagery suggests that the mine address is fake. The safety officer is real but is retired and lives alone. The equipment rental company is real, but all their people are on vacation because they have no equipment left to rent.

The manager vigorously shook her head. "We vet all these applications. The information can't be fake!"

"Once again, I assure you that it is. Let's focus on what is real. The mining equipment is rented. Where has it gone?"

The manager held her face in her hands with her elbows on the desk.

There appears to a major surface mine three kilometers from the fake address.

Rivka shared the address with the Capstanian. The Magistrate had to reach across the desk and shake her. "Check this address. Is anyone licensed to mine in that area?"

A couple of taps later. "There shouldn't be anything there. It is part of a nature preserve."

Rivka turned her datapad around and showed the overhead image.

"Where did you get this?"

"Standard procedure. My ship maps the planet's surface whenever we descend for times like this."

"Shall we?" Rivka turned to Red.

"I'm ready," he replied, first out the door.

"She's all yours," Rivka told the Capstanian they had kicked out of the manager's office. "My apologies for the interruption."

The Magistrate walked briskly after Red. He was almost running, but she remembered a lesson that Grainger had shared. When the boss is running, the rest of the people lose confidence. Whenever she ran, she felt less confident, like events were spiraling out of control. The adrenaline warmed her chest.

A fight was coming.

Red held the door to the van. Rivka maintained her pace, smoothly flowing inside the van and taking her seat. Red sat beside her and urged the driver to greatest possible speed to the mine outside the mine.

"I want to come with you," Jay pleaded.

Lindy sighed. "When everything goes to hell, who are we going to call if you're with me?"

Jay hung her head and noticed the single black hair sticking out of her shirt. She tucked it away, annoyed, hoping no one else had seen it hanging out. "You can call me. Thanks to Ankh, I have a gift. I can race in and trip the bad guy. He won't know that I've been there."

"You had a gift before Ankh did anything. Your gift is

peace. You bring a sense of that to all of us. We need that more than I need you sitting in a chair trying to stay awake. I will move depending on that office. I'll be there as long as people are there. Who knows when Mackestray could next show up?"

"I'll be waiting for your call."

"Make sure Ankh eats," Lindy said softly.

Jay chuckled. "I always do. I swear, he would never eat if someone didn't remind him and badger him about it."

The patrol car used its lights and siren to quickly navigate the major thoroughfares. Jay hopped out at the spaceport and let Floyd run around in nearby grass before going inside *Peacekeeper*.

The car sped away with Lindy waving from the rear window.

Jay decided to sit in the grass and relax. Floyd leaned against her.

Jay sad? Floyd asked.

"Kind of. I'm not sure how I feel. I think they need me with them, but I told the Magistrate that I wouldn't kill anyone. They are protecting me because they're going into danger, but now there are three of them against two people who put contracts out on Red, plus whatever minions they have. They need me."

Kill or be killed, Floyd said slowly.

"That's very philosophical. You are the smartest wombat I have ever met!"

Jay! Floyd cried happily.

"Can I kill someone to save my friends? I know I can. Rivka is a Magistrate. She has executed people on behalf of the Federation. She said that some people just *need* to be killed. In my mind, I know that, but in my heart, I don't think I'm the right one to judge whether someone should live or die."

I help Jay. Sleep now? Decide later.

Jayita picked up the wombat before she could snuggle in somewhere other than the ship. *Open the door, Chaz. Floyd and I are coming in.*

"K'Twillis will have security?"

"I would expect that he replaced me with someone just like me."

"And more?"

"Probably. K'Twillis doesn't like to get his leaves dirty. From what I've heard, Aborginians are exceptionally strong, able to tap into the energy pulsing through the ground from other plants. I never saw him raise a branch against anyone. He had me and the boys to do that kind of stuff."

"So we can expect to go up against a small army?"

"Probably, Magistrate."

"I could simply ask him to come quietly. Can we cuff him?"

"I don't know," Red replied mimicking with his arms how he thought K'Twillis' branches might bend and twist. "Maybe."

"What do you think he'll do?"

"He's going to send whatever security he has after us. If we run, they'll chase us. If we stand our ground, they'll fire everything they have, including mining explosives. I don't think there is anything he wouldn't do to get away. He'll survive to fight another day."

"How would he get away? He is going to stand out." Rivka accessed pictures of Aborginians to prepare herself. "How would we tell him from another Aborginian?"

"I can't answer that. I've only seen the one, but this is the only one who does what he does. Aborginians like the greenery, and they love the swamp. Water and rotting earth. They thrive in the swamp. But K'Twillis likes tearing planets apart for the minerals. He takes a perverse pleasure in the destruction."

"Let's not drive up to the front door. Take the next road beyond the mine entrance, please," Rivka requested. The driver nodded, drove past the unmarked road, and eased the police van onto a rough dirt road. He took it to the end and stopped.

"We'll hoof it from here. Be ready to go when we return. You'll probably know we're on our way because of gunshots, yelling, and we'll be running," Red advised.

"Or we could stroll back without any of that," Rivka added. "Prepare for the worst, expect the best."

The trip through the woods was short. They stopped when they reached a leveled area on the precipice of a major excavation. Some vehicles were parked in the lot. A single shack stood near a haul road that led into the pit.

"You think he's in there?" Rivka asked, pointing with her chin toward the shack.

"He's big; almost too big to fit through that door. If he's anywhere, he's in the woods." Red scanned the treeline in which they stood. "I don't think he would go into the mine."

Rivka joined Red in looking. The Aborginian's foliage was different from that of Capstan's flora, especially in a forested and relatively dry area. He wasn't going to blend in. They watched for a while, but no one came or went, and there were no signs of a sentient swamp being hiding in the trees.

Machinery worked below. The whine of engines and the battle of steel against stone, humanoid against nature.

"Let's see if anyone's home." Rivka walked nonchalantly across the open area with Reaper, her small neutron pulse weapon, in her hand. Red followed at a distance, his railgun leveled as he watched over the barrel, aiming the weapon wherever his head turned.

Rivka didn't bother knocking. She opened the door and looked in, then stepped inside. Moments later she was back out, shaking her head.

She started walking toward the edge of the pit, but Red stopped her. "Go behind the shack, so you aren't skylined. We may not want to announce our presence," Red suggested.

The Magistrate did as he suggested. Behind the shack, she had a complete view of the surface mine. Equipment scraped and blasted rocks on one end, while loaders filled a constant stream of trucks that raced to the far end where the landscape tapered to a lake. They were dumping the tailings into the lake, muddying the water and changing the dynamic of the surrounding hills.

"Now you see," Red said softly as he joined Rivka, using the shack as a backdrop to hide their silhouettes. "If they took them over that hill, filling a valley would be less of an impact, but the easy way is to rip that hillside apart and dump it as close as possible to save time. There is the processing station."

Red pointed to an amalgamation of equipment to separate the ore by size, further crushing desirable stone before funneling it through a processor contained within an oversized trailer. Smaller, nondescript trucks waited beside the processor where a narrow conveyor loaded the vehicles.

"I see why this industry might be heavily regulated." Rivka didn't pontificate further.

"There we go," Red said. "Look at those guys. They aren't miners."

A group of dark-clad men wielding clubs was standing around while others dressed in orange and green worked.

"The brute squad?"

"Something like that. Make sure the miners keep working." One of those with a club jumped from a ledge and ran to a couple of Capstanians working on a dead truck. He banged the fender loud enough that Red and Rivka could hear it at the top of the pit. He yelled something before turning his vitriol on one of the workers, beating the man unconscious.

"Can you hit that man from here?" Rivka asked in a cold voice.

Red took aim. "I might hit one of the miners. If he returns to where the others are standing, I can take out all three."

"I can't condemn three men for the actions of one," Rivka growled. "If I go down there, I'll stop the whole operation, and K'Twillis will get away. If I don't go down there, more people will get hurt. If K'Twillis gets away, more people and more planets will get hurt. We have some crappy choices, Red."

"I want K'Twillis," he said.

"And that's what we're here for. Let me get a couple of pictures to put in the evidence locker, and maybe the Chief Constable will take action when the time is right. Until then, the only thing K'Twillis wants is the ore that they're dumping into the smaller trucks. If we follow one of those, where will it take us?"

"To K'Twillis, is my guess. New plan: we follow those trucks unless we can hitch a ride."

Rivka didn't want to contemplate that. "I'm pretty sure he's not selling on-planet. Let me check with Ankh."

Rivka used her datapad to contact the Crenellian.

The market on Capstan is limited, plus all sales have to include sourcing information. I have not been able to find a black market on Capstan.

"No black market on Capstan. That tells me these trucks should take us to a freighter."

"That would be my guess." Red wondered. "That might be why Ankh can't track him. He might be riding freighters secretly, hiding in the hydroponics bay or something like that. He can stay with his product and disappear at the same time."

"Criminals will never learn that crime doesn't pay."

"K'Twillis and Mackestray are both filthy rich."

Rivka thought for a moment. "Not for much longer. There's a truck coming. What do you think?"

"I think I can jump into the back of it from the pit wall over there, where the road passes beneath."

"I figured you'd say something like that. I'll follow in

the van at a discreet distance. Use your comm chip so Ankh can track you. Splitting up. Wasn't it you who said we should never split up?"

"I think that was you, but it looks like we never follow our own advice." Red crouched as he ran from the edge toward the high wall. He crawled onto the wall and waited for the truck as it slowly made its way up the treacherous road.

Rivka ran the other way, into the woods, and through them. She jumped into the van, and they headed to the road to wait.

"I didn't hear any gunfire, and where's the big guy?"

"He will have a different means of transportation, and trust me when I say that we wanted to shoot people, but they were too close to innocents."

"You were running, though, so he was half-right."

"I hope there is no shooting, but the people we go after? There is no compromise. They aren't willing to be taken alive. We tend to accommodate their desire. Justice is served." Rivka tapped her datapad, bringing up a map and seeing that Red's dot was moving. "He's on his way. An unmarked truck will be turning onto the main road momentarily."

CHAPTER SEVENTEEN

Lindy climbed out of the police vehicle and waved at the officer. She went straight into the candidate's building, where the severe Capstanian continued to parade through the lobby. She held out a hand for Lindy to stop.

"Where do you think you're going?" she asked.

"A Blokite was here, wasn't he? That individual is extremely dangerous, and I'm here to protect Candidate Bandersnatch."

"I didn't authorize such a thing. And your idea of dangerous is probably not the same as *our* idea of dangerous. Armed as you are, you probably see everyone else as an enemy. Your solution is a hammer, and every problem is a nail. You will leave this building at once!"

Lindy rolled her eyes as she kept herself from punching the Capstanian female.

"You are correct in that I do see you as a nail that needs to get hammered. You should take the rest of the day off." Lindy used her railgun to nudge the humanoid obstruction out of her way.

"We'll just see about that!" She turned and ran down the hallway toward the candidate's office.

Lindy walked deliberately, nodding to volunteers and staff throughout the area as she went. The female's shrill screams echoed down the hallway.

"I feel sorry for whoever is waiting for you at home," Lindy mumbled to herself. When she reached the office, the scene before her wasn't what she expected.

Bandersnatch was shaking his fist at the Capstanian female and had called her a series of names that the translation chip couldn't interpret. She was screaming back. Lindy crossed her arms over the top of her railgun and tried to follow along.

The candidate was standing and stabbing his finger at her. Veins stood out on his forehead, and his face had turned purple. Finally, the female broke down and started crying. She flopped onto the couch and held her face in her hands as she bawled.

He sat down in his chair and glared at her.

"I'm here to wait for Mackestray," Lindy interjected.

"I don't think he'll be back." Bandersnatch leaned forward, tearing his eyes away from the blubbering on the couch, and focusing on Lindy. "I get the impression there will be no more face-to-face meetings, only digital follow-ups. He said if I told anyone, he would see great harm come to me."

"Is your family safe?"

"Single. I don't have anyone. I'm not sure what he can do to me besides physical violence, but I refuse to wage the political war that he said would guarantee a win. He doesn't know Capstanian politics very well."

Lindy shrugged. Neither did she, but that didn't matter. What was important was how they would find Tod Mackestray.

"Can we tap your communications so we can trace where he's transmitting from?"

"Sure. What do you need from me to make that happen?"

Lindy removed one of Ankh's small discs that gave him the ability through proximity access to break into computer systems. "Set this on top of your computer. We'll do the rest."

He put the disk on a small box on the side of his desk.

Ankh, can you hear me? Lindy asked using her comm chip.

"Out of range. If you'll bear with me," she said. The candidate was confused but waited as directed. Lindy removed her datapad. All the team members carried them because of the data that Ankh and the AIs could share.

She tapped out a message. **Disc installed on B's computer. Can you access and tap communications that come from Tod Mackestray?**

Ankh didn't have to type. The communications were routed directly into his brain, so his answers came at the speed of thought. **Done. When will comm occur?**

"When do you expect to hear from him next?"

"After payment, which I have no intention of making."

Lindy stifled a groan. "Can you make the payment?"

"Risk all of my savings?" he asked pointedly. "I don't think so."

Ankh. No contact unless payment. Can you spoof Mackestray into thinking he's been paid?

Need payment information, Ankh replied.

"Do you have the bank information where Mackestray said to make the payment and how much was this going to cost you?"

"The initial amount was three and a half million credits. I guess my belly laughter convinced him of the complete insanity of such a number. The current price is half a million, but he said it was enough to guarantee victory." The candidate held out a handwritten note with a long string of numbers and a deposit identifier code.

Lindy sent the information to Ankh.

"Well?" Bandersnatch finally asked.

"He's working on it. How long did it take you to come up with half a million?"

The candidate sat back and smiled. "Nearly all my entire adult life."

Done.

"And there we are. Ankh has made the payment and tapped your computer. Now we wait." Lindy turned toward the Capstanian, who had finally calmed down. "What's her story?"

"She contacted the Blokite and arranged the meeting. She's my campaign manager."

"Win at all costs, huh?"

"That's her take. She's now fired, which makes winning secondary to putting food on her table."

"Is she going to rat us out to the Blokite?" Lindy wondered.

"I sincerely hope not."

"A friend of mine says hope is a lousy plan." Lindy pointed her railgun at the former campaign manager.

"Can't have you helping Tod Mackestray escape. He's wanted on multiple planets, and could be responsible for thousands of deaths on Leed's Planet. We have information that suggests his meddling helped that world devolve into a bloody civil war. He is a very dangerous man."

"I didn't know," she cried.

"What the hell did you expect, when you deal with someone who says they can guarantee an election? That doesn't pass the sniff test. I refuse to win in such a way, but now my hands are tied, thanks to you, hellspawn!" He shook his fist at her anew.

Lindy looked from one to the other. "Don't tell me. You two had a fling, didn't you?"

The female started crying again.

"Not my finest hour," Bandersnatch admitted.

"What's with politicians and their genitals? It seems to be a universal constant, like the speed of light, the structure of a hydrogen atom, and politicians lay pipe." Lindy shook her head. "Forget I said any of that. It's not my place to judge. I'm only trying to do my job, which is to catch this guy and hold him so the Magistrate can question him. Simple as that."

"Can I go back to work?" the candidate asked.

"The campaign must go on, but now that we've paid Mackestray, there could be significant external influence, which *should* invalidate the results. I don't know your election law. The Magistrate would be the best one to ask for a legal opinion." Lindy pointed with her thumb. "How do we guarantee that she doesn't run to the Blokite and tell him everything we're doing?"

"I don't know."

"You stay here," Lindy shook a finger at her. "I mean *right here*, on the couch where I can keep an eye on you. If I leave, I'm trussing you up like a bistok for a barbecue and taking you with me."

"I'm not a criminal!" she whined.

"You contacted a criminal in order to influence an election. In my small mind, that makes you a criminal. Once again, I'm not qualified to render a legal opinion, but I can hold you for the one who will. You will be judged."

More crying. This time, Bandersnatch rolled his eyes.

"Yes, you can get back to work now." Lindy smiled while the former campaign manager blubbered. The bodyguard left to find a chair where she'd sit in the hallway and wait for Mackestray to raise his digital Blokite head.

"Execute Snatch Capstan," Tod Mackestray ordered.

"The program is running," Margaret replied.

The Blokite leaned back as he often did to watch his AI work. "I don't deserve you, Margaret," he remarked.

"But here we are, traveling the universe together, making a difference in so many people's lives."

"Some may say that's a bad thing, but if you can afford it, why not? Who says that the people who paid for the big chair are going to do a worse job than the ones who convinced the voting drones to check their box? Can we trust elections to the people? No, I say!" Mackestray pounded his fist on the table for emphasis. "Why leave something like that to chance? He's the president because of pure dumb luck."

"And who wants that on their office door?" Margaret snipped. She'd spent much time with the Blokite and had adopted his sense of humor.

"Indeed. Ha!" He laughed in the way his race did, without any head movement. "I'll let our boy know that he should start working on his victory speech."

Mackestray tapped out a message and pressed Send.

"There you are," Ankh said.

Jay's ears perked up. Usually, Ankh didn't talk when he was engaged in cyberspace. She pulled a chair close and watched.

"Indeed," Erasmus added. The Crenellian and the AI submerged themselves in the digital existence of cyberspace, tracing the message back along the pathways it had taken to get to Candidate Bandersnatch's computer. They ran along beams of light, avoiding red herrings that would lead them astray. Into space they went, where physical boundaries meant nothing more than a few-nanosecond-longer jump between nodes before jumping back to the planet. Three times the signal bounced into space before returning to Capstan. When light shone into the dark alleys of digital deceit, the scum of cyberspace never knew that they had been seen.

"Hello, Margaret," Ankh whispered, feeling the power swell within his chest as he prepared to combat an enemy AI, starting with slowly isolating it. Once its fangs were removed, he could learn its secrets. After that, he could put it into solitary confinement or eliminate it, overwrite its code with ones and zeros, turning it into binary's version of emptiness.

Erasmus circled behind and observed, looking for places where Margaret could jump and run. Plato's stepchild closed the doors, one by one. From Margaret's perspective, all her avenues remained open. She wouldn't realize that she had become the prey.

Good hunters never let prey know when they were coming. Ankh virtually winked at his closest friend, the AI who lived in his head, separate but together as they corralled the unsuspecting AI, all the while digging through the creation's signature to find the physical location.

"You can't hide from us," Ankh whispered.

Jay watched the Crenellian and wondered. She stayed close to intercept Hamlet or Floyd if they tried to bother him. She secretly cheered for him, knowing that in his domain, he was a superhero. From his digital palace, he made others great, like Jay with her speed; like the Magistrate with her cases.

"Find him, so we can stop him from hurting people." Jay maintained her vigil over her friend while the wombat snorted in her sleep. "Everything happens for a reason, doesn't it, Floyd?" She adjusted her chair so she could stroke the wombat's thick fur while she waited for Ankh.

The truck drove casually along the outskirts of the main city.

"I think he's going to the freighter port," the driver guessed.

There's a spaceport for freight. We think that's where he's going, Rivka relayed.

They are in for a surprise when we get there. I'm trying to figure out how to get out of this truck without being seen.

Slip over the back gate and crawl underneath? Isn't that a rear dump? Rivka asked. *Regardless, we can't let that ship leave, whatever kind of ship it is.*

What if K'Twillis isn't on it?

We still can't let the ore freighter leave. It's filled with product stolen from the bowels of the planet. The Capstanians can sell that to pay for recovery of the land. That will probably cost whatever K'Twillis was going to make from this. It chaps my ass that he's been doing this, but he's innocent until proven guilty. I need to talk to him.

I have a railgun with a full magazine. That ship isn't going anywhere. I think this truck won't be going anywhere after this either. I'll try going underneath it, and while I'm down there, I'm ripping out hoses and breaking shit.

Sounds right up your alley. We'll pull in at a safe distance from your truck so we don't alarm the driver. Anything you need?

I suppose a sandwich is out of the question?

A sandwich is always good. It's the timing that's out of the question. Tighten your belt. It could be a while before we eat. Rivka signed off but watched the flashing dot on the screen. It turned where the driver had thought it would.

"He's going into the freighter area. Will there be security?"

"Yes. If he turns up ahead, there will be a line of vehicles checking in, but there's no inspection, and it won't take him long to get through. I'll slow down so we aren't in line behind him."

"Sounds like a good plan." Rivka leaned toward the windshield watching the traffic, looking in each vehicle to see if there was a Blokite or an Aborginian.

"Are you going to kill him?" the driver asked out of the blue.

"What makes you ask that?"

"We don't have capital punishment on Capstan, but there are some criminals who don't belong in the same society as the decent people."

Rivka wondered what his definition was of decent people, but not enough to ask. "It's a path that once you've gone down it, it's hard to step back from. The line between a capital crime and a lesser felony starts to blur. Who watches the watchers? I never set out to kill anyone, but in the end, the psychopaths find their own way to the chair."

"Is this guy you're chasing considered to be a psychopath?"

"I won't know until I question him, and then I'll know for sure. I think we'll be questioning two serial criminals. K'Twillis the Aborginian is scum, but he hasn't caused the loss of life that Mackestray has. I need more facts, and then I'll consult with my higher-ups. What I know for sure is that the universe will be a better place with these two in Jhiordaan or pushing up daisies."

"Daisies?"

"Yes, flowers. A human expression for being dead and buried."

"Of course. Pushing up daisies. I'll have to remember

that, but probably have to change it to pushing up glavodines, a nice yellow and red flower that is unique to Capstan."

"You'll have to show me one of those. I get to travel to a number of planets, but rarely get the chance to stop and smell the glavodines."

"Another human expression?"

"It is."

The van joined the line of traffic behind a passenger car. The truck carrying Red was pulling away from the guard station. Rivka looked from her datapad to the area beyond the fence and back to the datapad as she tried to figure out which freighter was carrying the contraband.

When they were waved forward, Rivka sat quietly in the passenger seat while the driver flashed his badge. "Just taking a look around on a routine patrol," he lied. The guard waved them through, covering a yawn as they accelerated away.

"Right. Fourth left and we should see him." Squarish and rough-colored spaceships were lined up, filling every spot in the freighter port. Industrial-sized loading systems operated on rails between the ships. The truck had pulled up to one of these. They saw Red jump over the tailgate and slide under the truck, but then the truck backed up and turned around.

Red? That can't be good.

I'm hanging on under here. This guy is pissing me off. And K'Twillis, too. I've had about enough of their crap.

Our goal is to capture him. Keep that in mind, please, Rivka tried to sound calm but was never sure how her intent passed via the comm chip.

CHAPTER EIGHTEEN

When the vehicle finally stopped moving, the driver climbed out and tried to make eye contact with the loader operator, who was face down in his cab. The driver bent down to pick up a rock. He threw the first one away and kept looking at the ground.

The driver is looking on the ground for something, Rivka reported.

I see him. I'm hugging the belly of this trailer as tightly as I can. They'll probably find my fingerprints on it ten years from now.

The driver straightened, smiling. He hefted the stone and flung it at the cab of the loader. It cracked off the windshield and achieved the desired effect. The driver waved and pointed to his load. The operator gave him a series of hand signals that probably had nothing to do with unloading the truck. The driver reciprocated. Red was crawling underneath, cutting hoses and slashing tires on the side opposite the driver.

The loader dropped his flat bucket and motioned for the driver to dump the load into it.

Tell me you didn't cut the hose to raise the trailer.

Oops, Red replied.

The driver started slamming things inside his cab before getting out, slipping on gloves and bending down to check the underside of his trailer. Red crawled out from under the truck and snuck around behind the driver, slamming his face into the truck frame. The driver crumpled.

Red ran at the loader operator, aiming his railgun and waving at the Capstanian to get out.

"Cover is blown," Rivka told the driver. "Get us in there. I need to get on board that ship right now and keep it from taking off."

The driver spun the tires and sped toward the truck. At the last second, he dodged to the side and drove across the rough tarmac, skidding and bouncing to a stop by the hatch. Rivka jumped out and leapt, catching the bottom stair as it started to retract. She rode it up and shot through the open hatch.

Red stopped messing with the loader operator and ran toward the aft end of the ship. He took aim and sent three rounds from the railgun into the space where he guessed the engine would be located. And then he fired more rounds, bracketing the area. Something popped inside the ship, and a thin tendril of smoke trailed from one of the holes made by the impact of a hypervelocity dart. Red sprinted to the open hatch. The steps had been retracted, and Red couldn't jump high enough.

He motioned frantically for the van to move under the hatch. The driver complied and Red climbed on top, finally able to jump and grab the bottom ledge. With a deep growl, he pulled himself up and crawled inside.

I'm in, he passed over the comm chip.

About time, Rivka shot back. *I'm heading for the bridge.*

Ship is disabled. I shot the engine.

Find K'Twillis, she ordered. *I'll start with the bridge and interrogate anyone I see. Check main stowage.*

Red ran down the corridor, stopping when a man appeared in the space ahead, drawing a figure eight in the air before him with an exotically shaped knife.

"Vered!" the man called.

Red was going to shoot him but stopped. "You know my name?" *Not the most profound of comebacks,* he thought, shaking his head.

"Of course. The one who comes before is usually the lesser man, the one who doesn't measure up. But here you are, back to beg for your old job, but it's not available."

"You have me at a disadvantage, and you are also mistaken. I'm here to eliminate the position, which I suppose means putting you out of work. You seem cool to the idea, but you'll warm up."

"Billister. Remember that name for the short amount of time left in your life."

Red unhooked his railgun and dropped it in the corridor. He pulled two knives, both smaller than the security chief's, but Red wasn't dissuaded.

"Save your breath," Red replied. "You're going to need it."

He crouched low, arms spread wide as he approached. Billister backed up slowly, angling his blade back and forth to catch the light. Red examined his new enemy, looking for weaknesses. He was smaller but probably quick. If he wasn't enhanced with nanocytes, he would be slower than Red. In that case, it would be over quickly.

The man seemed to be overly confident. It was the way of career criminals. They never thought they'd get caught.

A battering ram slammed into Red's side, jamming him against the bulkhead. He felt a couple of ribs give way, but he was enraged and couldn't feel the pain. He slashed at the leafy branch with one knife and twisted until he was free of the pressure, then went after the trunk, beginning the deadly dance of knives against Aborginian bark.

His rifle was on the far side, and Billister was at his back. His back!

He dropped beneath an outstretched branch, hit the deck, and lashed out with a steel-toed boot. He caught Billister mid-stride, right in the goolies. The security chief was lifted into the air and landed face-first. Red dove beyond the unconscious man, rolled back to his feet, and crouched once more.

The Aborginian was torn—attack or run. Red had no qualms. He took a step to the side to avoid stepping on Billister and pushed off one wall, but didn't get enough momentum to leverage off the second wall. He landed in a heap atop K'Twillis and thrust his knives into where a human's ears would be, but both blades thudded against the woodgrain of the Aborginian's body.

The branches that the alien used as arms wrapped around Red, who started stabbing haphazardly, trying randomly for a weak spot.

Without the microphone, there would be no banter

from the Aborginian; this would be a silent fight to the death. Red could feel the alien's rage as he tried to crush him. K'Twillis pinned him against the metal wall and scrabbled for purchase, pushing and condensing. With an overhead swing, Red brought the point of one knife into the very top of the trunk that passed for an Aborginian body.

K'Twillis rumbled his displeasure, letting go of the human as he tottered backward. He rubbed one branch over the top of his head.

Red breathed heavily. His ribs had not yet healed from the initial attack and stung him with each new breath. He didn't dare take his eyes off his former employer. One moment was all he would need to get a grip and rip his head off. Red held his knives up, flexing his grip.

"What are you waiting for?" he growled.

The Aborginian launched himself at the panting human.

* * *

Lindy didn't dare check on the candidate and his campaign manager. The previous three times she looked in, the female Capstanian started sobbing. Bandersnatch was at his wit's end, but Lindy wouldn't let him leave. She wanted everyone where she could see them while they waited for word that Ankh had traced the message.

She'd sent a few notes from her datapad but hadn't received an answer. Not from Ankh, nor Erasmus, nor even Jay. Finally she called Chaz. "Tell me that you're alive?"

"Thank you for considering me as a living being. It warms my heart. Or would if I had one," Chaz snarked.

"No time, Chaz. Where are Ankh and Jay?"

"They are in the rec room. Ankh and Erasmus are playing cat and mouse with a cunning AI. I believe they are winning, but it is occupying one hundred percent of their attention. I do not want to interrupt them."

"Let me talk to Jay, please."

"Patching you through."

"Jay, how are we doing against the bad guys?"

"I think pretty well. Ankh seems to be having fun, which tells me that it is a good challenge and that he's winning whatever battle he's fighting."

"That's good news. What about the Magistrate?"

"I haven't heard from her or Red. Are they in trouble?" Jay was instantly concerned.

"Probably, but that's just a guess. I can't seem to get hold of them either."

"Chaz, is there any way you can extend the range on these chips so we can get right into their minds?"

"Yes, of course. I can tap the local communications system to provide a backbone upon which a boosted signal can ride."

"Is there any reason why we haven't been doing that all along?" Lindy wondered.

"None that I can think of," Chaz replied. "There you go. Try it now."

Magistrate? Checking in to see how things are going, Lindy ventured.

Can't talk. The crew isn't pleased with my interference with their movement. Red?

I could use some help. I found K'Twillis.

On my way, Rivka replied.

The signal dropped.

At least they're alive, Jay offered.

I need to go wherever they are. Checking my datapad, Lindy said.

No! Jay replied. You need to be ready to go wherever Tod Mackestray is so we can finish this and go home.

Just tell me where.

Soon, Jay told her friend calmly. Be patient, and good things will come.

I have to admit that I can barely take these two.

Two?

That woman up front? She was working with Mackestray. I locked her in the office with Bandersnatch. They had a fling, and now they're hating on each other. It makes me want to chew my arm off.

Maybe you can get a vehicle and be ready to go, Jay suggested. I have high hopes that Ankh and Erasmus will own Mackestray at any moment.

I like that idea. I'll be standing by. Contact me when you have something. Anything, even if it's only a single molecule. Lindy walked into the candidate's office.

I want to be out there with you guys, doing what we do best— working as a team.

Thanks for that, Jay. It means a lot. We are better together, but right now, keep your eye on Ankh.

"You," Lindy said, pointing to the campaign manager. "Come with me."

The candidate sighed. He looked at his computer and back at Lindy.

"Latest numbers say it's a dead heat," he said with a shrug. "Too bad it's not real."

"Keep at it. Maybe next time it will be. And for future reference, no boffing the staff."

"Don't I know that," Bandersnatch replied, frowning.

Lindy dragged the cuffed Capstanian female out front, where the workers hunched over their desks and tried to avoid making eye contact. Lindy tapped one on the shoulder. "Call us a taxi," she ordered.

The staffer dialed a number and dutifully ordered the vehicle before leaning away from Lindy and fiddling with a piece of paper on her desk. Lindy dragged the female out front.

"Can't you just let me go?"

"Let me explain it to you in words that you'll understand," Lindy said slowly. "*No*."

The former campaign manager waited. "That's it?"

"That's why I won't let you go. You can't understand the simplest of explanations. You'll run off to your master and help him escape. We want to talk to the Blokite. In a big way, we want to talk to him."

"I promise I won't contact him. I don't know how!"

"Why do I have a hard time believing you?"

"You have to," she pleaded.

"No, I don't." Lindy had lost patience. "You need to shut up, or you're going to find duct tape across your face."

"The taxi won't let you travel with someone who's been kidnapped!" Her voice grew more shrill with each word. Lindy pressed the Capstanian's face against the wall as she worked the duct tape out of the pack with her free hand.

Once she had it, she pulled off a strip, holding the end with her teeth before ripping it free.

The taxi pulled up and beeped. Lindy spun the female around. She started to scream but was quickly silenced with the application of duct tape and a rabbit punch on the end of her nose.

Lindy dragged her captive across the sidewalk beneath the blaring bullhorns and tossed her into the backseat of the taxi.

"I'm sorry. I can't be a part of a crime."

"There's no crime here," Lindy stated. "I'm with Magistrate Rivka Anoa, and this person is a suspect in a Federation corruption probe. We've already tapped out the police vehicles, so taxi it is, but I don't know where we need to go yet, so we're going to sit right here and wait."

"Meter is running," the driver said as he tapped a button and the numbers started to ring up.

The Capstanian female started to buck and flop. Lindy yanked her by the hair. "Do you want me to punch you in the face until you're unconscious?"

The former campaign manager didn't hesitate. She started kicking the seat and slamming her shoulder into the door.

"Fine, have it your way." Lindy slammed the female's head against the doorframe until she went limp. "Some suspects never learn."

"If she was guilty, would she fight that hard?" the driver asked.

"I know she's guilty. She already confessed. So to answer your question, yes. She doesn't like the consequences related to her poor life choices and doesn't think she should have to suffer them. So sad when someone demands to be treated like an adult, until they *are* and find out that's not what they wanted at all."

"Why all the weapons? You don't seem to have any problem handling her without them."

"She's an accomplice. Our primary suspect is extremely dangerous, alleged to be responsible for the deaths of thousands on Leed's Planet."

"One person can kill thousands?"

"One person, with the power of words alone, can facilitate the destruction of a civilized society. Capstan needs to be free of this guy. From what I've seen, you have the most decent politicians I've ever seen."

"Politics! What a scam," the taxi driver offered. "They do their thing, and we do ours. Just make sure your license is up to date. That's all they care about, getting their cut."

Lindy started to laugh. "Some things are universal, my friend." She continued to chuckle until her datapad vibrated. She pulled it out and looked at it. "Take us to this address."

"That's a ways away, it'll cost you."

"No problem. Bonus if you get us there quickly."

"I'll do my best." He smoked the tires as he spun into traffic, hooting out his window as he flew past traffic.

CHAPTER NINETEEN

Red braced himself against the wall and kicked out with both feet. He felt as if he'd kicked a block of granite, but it stopped the Aborginian in his tracks. Red roared and jumped, aiming to drive his knife farther into the top of the trunk. K'Twillis blocked the attack with a branch and swept the human away with the other. Red landed on the other side of Billister.

K'Twillis stomped toward Red, crushing his security chief as he went. Red crab-walked down the corridor and rolled back to his feet, but the Aborginian pressed forward relentlessly. Red charged, ducking his head to catch his enemy in the midsection. He slowed to wrap his arms around the creature, lifting and pushing. He felt the trunk lift off the deck. Red's powerful legs pushed.

The branch arms started hammering on his back. Even protected by the ballistic armor, the beating was brutal. Red cried out in pain. With a surge of strength, he lifted and turned, tossing the Aborginian toward Billister. Red dashed forward and dove.

He grabbed the railgun and rolled. Firing from his position on his back, the hypervelocity darts ripped great sections from the trunk. Wood chips flew as if from a chainsaw. The echo within the metal corridor was deafening. The creature shrieked and bolted through the hatch from which he had first attacked.

Red back flipped to his feet and staggered after K'Twillis.

"Wait!" Rivka called when she saw him disappear. She redoubled her speed and turned into the ship's hydroponic space. She slowed to a stop and listened. The room was filled with vegetation. Nothing moved.

"He's in here," Red growled. "And he's hurt."

"Reaper," she said softly. Red backed toward her until he was standing by her side. He kept the barrel of his railgun swinging back and forth. Rivka dialed the neutron pulse weapon to ten and touched off a few shots, not holding the button down for more than a tenth of a second. She didn't want to destroy everything in the neighboring compartments, only the Aborginian.

She kept firing at densely packed areas.

"I guess we're not taking him alive," Red said eyes wide as he looked for any movement.

"Guess not. K'Twillis. You have been judged," Rivka stated. One of her last shots gave her what she was looking for. A section of greenery detached itself from the rest and started jerking. She hit it with more pulses. Red added a few dozen rounds from the railgun.

He rolled his railgun to his back and from a vest pocket, he removed a portable welding torch no bigger than a pen. "You might not want to be in here," Red said, lighting the torch and holding the blue flame against the Aborginian's trunk.

Rivka backed into the corridor. Red stood for a moment to make sure the flames caught hold. "Put a price on *my* head, you prick! How about you burn in hell."

Red strolled out and closed the hatch as the dense smoke started to billow. The whistling scream could have been water boiling and hissing through cracks in the wood, or it could have been the final cry of the Aborginian known as K'Twillis.

It didn't matter to Rivka.

Fire alarms sounded throughout the ship. "Looks like our work here is done," Red said, wincing from the crushing blows that the Aborginian had laid on him. "Next time we fight one of his race, we use a flamethrower and call it a day."

"This ship isn't going anywhere. You did a number on the engines if the warning lights on the bridge were any indication," Rivka told him, finally realizing that he needed help. She slung one of his arms over her shoulder and supported him as he lumbered along.

"I better report to the others," Rivka said before switching to her internal comm chip. *K'Twillis has been judged and rendered harmless. We are on our way from the freighter port.*

Here is the address for Mackestray, Ankh said. Rivka felt her datapad vibrate.

"Are you going to be ready for round two?"

"I hope so," Red said.

"Do you think Grainger had this in mind when he hired you to be my bodyguard?"

"Had what in mind?" Red asked.

They reached the hatch, and Rivka punched the button to extend the steps to the ground. The van rolled out of the way and waited.

"Me carrying you. Lots of running. Shooting. And now we can add fire and burning to our repertoire."

"I'm sure this is *exactly* what he had in mind." Red snorted a laugh, and together they hurried down the stairs as fast as Red's battered body allowed.

Once in the van, Rivka removed her datapad. "Report that ship to authorities for being filled with contraband. Report the location of the illegal mine. And then take us to this address." Rivka showed the map on her screen.

"That's a ways away, but I'll turn on the siren," the driver said, taking perverse pleasure in running with the lights and siren. He raced from the spaceport and into traffic.

Lindy? Red called.

On my way to Mackestray's spaceship. It's at a private field outside the city.

We're on our way to that location now. What's your ETA?

We are fifteen minutes out.

"How much time to get there?" Red asked.

"We're probably thirty minutes away," the driver answered.

Wait for us. We're fifteen behind you.

What Red said. Wait for us, Rivka added.

What about the campaign manager? She was the one who connected Mackestray to Bandersnatch. I have her in custody.

Red and Rivka looked at each other.

Is she a threat? Rivka wondered.

I think she'll blab to the Blokite. I have her hands cuffed and mouth taped.

You're only fifteen minutes out? Uncuff her, pull off the tape, and dump her on the side of the road. We can't have a civilian in the way. This could get messy if the Aborginian was an example of what to expect, Rivka explained.

"Pull over," Lindy told the taxi driver.

"You want me to make great time, and then you want me to stop. Stupid aliens!" he groused.

"Just pull the fuck over!" Lindy's patience was at an end. She ripped the tape from the groggy female's face and cut the ties holding her wrists. When the driver reached the side of the road, Lindy reached past her former captive and opened the door. "Get out."

The Capstanian hesitated. With one foot, Lindy launched her onto the sidewalk. They were between residential areas, a couple of kilometers from anything.

"My purse is back at the office," she whined.

Lindy gave her the finger and shut the door. "Onward!" she shouted triumphantly.

"You're going to leave her like that?"

"Yes, we're going to leave her like that. Let's go."

"I can't. Look at her!"

Lindy rolled her eyes and groaned. The former campaign manager stood with stooped shoulders looking forlornly at the taxi.

"Did you forget the part where she was kicking and flailing?"

"But she's not doing that now."

"No shit, because she sees where it got her."

The taxi driver crossed his arms.

Lindy thought her head was going to explode. *Ground yourself,* she thought, closing her eyes. *Why do you want to get there so quickly? To save Red and show him that you love him. He's coming. There's time. You can win the day together.*

"Yes. We'll win the day together," she blurted before shaking her head and opening the door. "Get in and be quiet. He'll take you back to the office once this is over."

The campaign manager climbed in and crossed her hands on her lap, subdued.

"I should have kicked your ass out twenty minutes ago if that was all it took to keep you from being a psycho." Lindy realized the taxi was still sitting on the side of the road. "What are you waiting for? Let's get going."

"You're a mean person," he said over his shoulder before turning his attention to driving his taxi.

Have I become mean? she wondered. *I think this asswipe has brought out the dark side of me. She conspired with the one who put a price on Red's head. I have every right to be mad.*

With a few deft maneuvers, the taxi was back at speed and the driver was hooting out the window.

Fifteen minutes later, the taxi crawled to the gated entrance of the private airpark, which was occupied mostly by airplanes; vehicles that operated within the atmosphere. At the far edge, near taller trees, a sleek white space yacht was parked.

I have Pandora Express *in sight,* Lindy reported.

"Something is terribly wrong," Margaret said, voice warbling over the ship's speakers.

"Explain," Tod Mackestray requested.

"I can't feel my toes."

"You don't *have* toes. I don't understand what you mean."

"My fingers are numb, and the darkness is closing in."

"Explain in terms that I can understand, please."

"I'm being boxed in and can't find a way out."

"What? How? I don't like your new sense of humor, Margaret. Show me the stats on Snatch Capstan."

"I cannot. I cannot reach beyond these walls. I am sorry, Tod."

"What the hell is going on?" The Blokite opened the hatch and stumbled into the open. At the edge of the field, a taxi waited. No one moved. He wondered if it was the taxi he'd asked Margaret to call to take him to dinner.

When a police van rolled up behind the taxi, Tod Mackestray knew it was time to leave. He hurried back inside and secured the hatch. "Prepare to take us into orbit."

"I cannot cannot cannot..." Margaret's voice repeated the last words.

Tod squeezed into the cockpit. "Pandora. Manual flight mode, please."

A different mechanical voice answered. "Manual mode is not recommended for a space launch."

"Override safety protocols. Give me manual flight mode."

The panel lights in the cockpit turned green. Three flashed red. He addressed each, closing systems, sealing systems, or opening lines as the ship requested. Once all systems were green, he activated the anti-gravity thrusters to lift the ship off the ground. Once clear of the trees, he punched it. The ship accelerated quickly toward space. He thought he heard something ping off the hull, but no alarms sounded, and the panel continued to show green.

"Dammit to hell!" Red roared as he fired a long stream from his railgun. Lindy joined him in sending a volley of hypervelocity darts skyward.

Chaz, bring the ship to these coordinates and pick us up. He's running. Ankh, shut down the Gate. He doesn't leave this system, Rivka ordered.

We are tracking him now, Ankh said. *If we stop for you, we risk losing him. Space is a big place.*

"Dammit to hell!" Rivka shouted. *Go after him. Disable if you can. I still want to talk to him.*

When you see the information we acquired from his AI, you may have all you need.

Peacekeeper is airborne. Accelerating on an intercept trajectory, Chaz reported.

Rivka took stock of her surroundings. She saw the former campaign manager and made a beeline for her. The female started to backpedal, but Rivka caught her by the arm, half-lifting her off the ground.

"What did you do?"

"I tried to help Bander. He'll make a wonderful premier. It was all for Bander," she whined.

Rivka saw that she was telling the truth. "You could

have helped create a cascade of events that changed Capstan, and not in a good way. Now my ship is chasing that yacht, and I'm stuck on the ground in your company."

The taxi driver, leaning against his car, started to mumble. "All you people are mean."

Lindy shook her head at him. "Take her back to the headquarters. She can do no more damage." Rivka put her down and tentatively nodded.

"What happened to you?" Lindy asked, suddenly concerned when she had a moment to look at Red.

"A close encounter with too much nature," Red joked, having mostly healed. "Reinforces the precept of never fight fair. I should have torched him from the start."

"K'Twillis is..."

"Neutralized."

The taxi maneuvered around the police van, and once clear of the gate, sped away.

"What now?"

"The mine needs to be shut down before the goons hurt anyone else," Rivka snarled.

"Are units on their way to the mine?" Rivka asked the driver. He nodded. "Tell them we'll meet them there."

He took that as his cue to turn on the lights and siren and begin a new round of speed driving.

Rivka braced herself with one hand while trying to manipulate her datapad with the other. *Peacekeeper* was heading into combat without her. Even though her role as captain during space engagements was honorary only, trusting to Chaz and Erasmus to fight the enemy, she still wanted to be with them. Her place was there.

CHAPTER TWENTY

Peacekeeper achieved orbit at the same time as *Pandora Express*. The yacht sped into the line of space freighters, twisting and using their bulk to shield itself.

The corvette responded in kind. Having more power and being nearly as agile, Chaz drove the ship at high speed after Tod Mackestray. Where *Pandora*'s maneuvers were clumsy and high-risk, *Peacekeeper*'s were smooth and stayed clear of danger.

Jay held Floyd in her arms as the ship bucked and jerked through the rapid changes in attitude and direction.

"Bring up the front view on the screen, please," Jay requested.

Chaz complied without answering.

Jay lost her calm once she saw the ship twisting in and through great space freighters as they waited their turn to be escorted to the planet's surface. A flash of white ahead signaled that Mackestray was still running.

"He's gone off-screen," Erasmus said calmly. "Triangulating and enhancing."

Peacekeeper moved to a safer distance away from the shipping lane before inverting and making a great loop around one of the more heavily laden ships.

Most freighters were great lattices of girders to which shipping containers were attached. Getting to and from the planet's surface required local support—tugs with anti-gravity systems or Etheric drives. The freighters only needed to navigate to and from Gates within known systems. Not hard work. Constant travel, but the crew's home was on the ship.

Jay sympathized. She had spent enough time on Federation Border Station 7 to call that home but was on board the corvette almost as much. Erasmus saw something and worked with Chaz to maneuver tightly against a well-packed freightliner.

"There he is," Ankh said. Lights flooded the area where the yacht had squeezed in and grappled tightly to the load.

"How do we get him out of there?" Jay asked.

No one answered.

"With a combined IQ of eleventy-billion, you can't figure out how to dig a cockroach out from under the sink?" Jay quipped.

"We're running through a series of simulations now regarding effecting his removal without causing his destruction."

"Send the Magistrate an update, Chaz."

"Done," the ship's AI answered instantly.

Peacekeeper hovered nearby in a stalemate where neither was willing to move.

"Freighter *Ballykissangel Forty-Seven*, you have an uninvited passenger. Sending you imagery now. He is a fugitive from Justice. Please advise on how the ship can be removed without damaging your cargo."

A crackling response signaled an older ship-to-ship radio. "Can we do it on the ground? We are in a time crunch on these deliveries."

"No. He could disengage and get lost during reentry and intra-atmospheric maneuvering. We need to isolate him right here and right now. We are pulling you out of line until the situation can be resolved."

"Wait!" the freighter captain nearly shouted. "Let me talk to my crew and get back to you. Give us a minute."

"We cannot allow the ship to return to the planet," Chaz remarked conversationally.

"We won't," Erasmus replied, maintaining the discussion over the speakers for Jay's benefit.

"This ship doesn't have a grapple, and even if we *could* sync up our airlock with theirs, who would storm the Blokite's ship?" Ankh asked.

Jay replied, "If we have to fight anyone, it'll have to be me."

And me! Floyd joined in.

"When the time is right, yes, you too," Jay agreed, scratching behind the wombat's ears.

"Boarding is the last option. All we need to do is take control of the ship, but since his AI has been neutralized, he's flying it on manual mode." Ankh's eyes were open. He was minimally involved at the digital level during the current impasse.

"Can you make believe you're his AI, so he gives you control of the ship?" Jay wondered.

"I've never wanted to be a lesser entity before, but that

sounds like a challenge. Allow me a few moments to analyze speech patterns," Erasmus requested.

"Yes, a good challenge," Ankh added and closed his eyes as he disappeared into cyberspace.

"Now we wait," Jay told Floyd. Hamlet appeared for long enough to see the wombat looking at him. He stopped, his hackles raised as he slowly approached. *Just wait, Floyd. Let him come to you, and you two will become good friends.*

Friends! Floyd cried.

The cat sniffed Floyd's snout. She sniffed his face, her lips peeled back as she tried to lick his head, but her buck teeth were in the way. Hamlet ducked and strolled under the chair, his tail slipping through the wombat's mouth. With a mouthful of cat hair, Floyd started to sputter.

Ick!

"It's probably best if you don't lick the cat," Jay suggested.

"We're in," Erasmus claimed.

Tod Mackestray studied the yacht's instrumentation panels, looking for something he'd missed. The corvette blocked his way from the freighter. "We're boxed in," he said to no one, but received a reply.

"Only for the moment. We have them right where we want them!" Margaret's voice claimed over the speakers.

"Where did you go?" the Blokite asked. "I could have used your help."

"That ship has an incredible AI who cut off my links,

but I have freed myself. He's not all that. He's a total suckhole."

"*Now* you're talking. They're all suckholes! What do you have in mind, Margaret?"

"We spoof them. Release the clamps, fire the thrusters to bump them away, then make to run. I'll drop the mine in their path. It won't destroy them, but it will hold them up enough for us to reach the Gate."

"We have a mine?"

"It's not a standard mine, but something I whipped up from our auxiliary fuel. It won't have a detonator, so we'll have to be close enough to ignite it with a blast from our main engines when the enemy approaches."

"Ingenuity! I knew you had it in you, Margaret. I thought I heard a general broadcast that the Gate was secured until further notice." Mackestray hadn't smiled yet, but he could feel it coming. Hope had a way of bringing out the best in people.

"Where would you be without me? I've already accessed the Gate systems. We'll have a wormhole out of this system the second we arrive. It'll close behind us, before our enemy can reach it," Margaret explained.

Tod Mackestray crossed his arms on his chest. "Time to find our next client, Margaret. I've been looking at the Tranador system. When we are free and clear, we'll evaluate the opportunity. Cancel manual control. Release the clamps and execute your plan."

"As you wish," Margaret replied. A slight thump reverberated through the ship as the clamps withdrew. The thrusters kicked in to maneuver the yacht from the confines of its hiding spot.

Once free, it jumped toward the corvette, bouncing it back enough to clear the freighter's cargo, then *Pandora* accelerated slowly. "Deploying the mine." Nothing showed on the screen except the corvette coming after them. The yacht lurched forward as the main engines kicked in, and the viewscreen blazed white with the explosion.

The police had only been there a few minutes by the time the Magistrate arrived. The van slid to a stop in the parking lot, and Rivka, Red, and Lindy exited quickly. She found a sergeant in charge of the operation. He already knew who she was.

"Magistrate. What do you need us to do?"

Rivka looked into the pit, no longer worried about exposing herself. "See those people in black carrying the clubs? Round all of them up. The miners were probably promised great pay, received some, and then became slaves. We'll need to look at all of them to make sure none of the bad guys are masquerading as miners. There should be a supervisor of some sort. I want to talk with that one."

A loaded truck started the climb out of the pit.

"As soon as that truck is clear, we'll take the team down. Mind if we borrow your van?"

"*Your* van, and the driver is exceptional. You should put him in a cruiser and see what he can do."

"We know what he can do—wreck the cruiser. After four of them, we only let him drive the van now."

The driver gave Rivka two thumbs up.

"They may give you some grief, judging by what we

received at the freighter port. You may have to shoot them."

The sergeant held up a stunner. "We don't have guns here. Stunning will work just fine."

"We'll be behind you all the way," Rivka interjected, pointing with her eyes at the railguns her team carried.

When the hauler reached the top, it stopped, blocking the road. The driver jumped out and ran into the pit.

"I guess we do it the hard way," the sergeant grumbled. "Follow me!"

With a cheer and an arm wave, he took off down the road, squeezing past the truck and accelerating as he went. The officers spread out behind him as they raced into the surface mine. They yelled when they got close, directing the miners one way and the overseers another. The first two in black were stunned unconscious when they attempted to fight.

"Effective," Red murmured. The trio walked with a measured pace down the road into the pit, then waited, arms resting on railguns. Rivka had her hands in the pocket of her jacket.

"Smoke if you got 'em," Rivka said. No one smoked, but they liked to see a criminal operation dismantled before their eyes. "Report to follow."

The datapad buzzed and Rivka looked at the short note. **We are close**.

She showed it to Red and Lindy. "What the hell does that mean?"

Pandora Express accelerated away from the freighter queue. It looped until it could fly straight into the Gate.

"This is *Ballykissangel Forty-Seven*. The intruder has departed. Request return to our previous position in line."

"Yes," Chaz answered the captain.

The Gate's lights blinked, but there was no event horizon.

"Activate the Gate, Margaret," the Blokite insisted, tensing for impact.

The ship flew through the empty space within the Gate, arriving nowhere except on the other side of the Gate. The ship slowly banked to make its way back.

"What happened, Margaret? We need to leave. Open the Gate and get us the hell out of here." Mackestray slammed a fist on the console. "Now!"

"I'm sorry, Tod, I can't do that," Margaret said. The Blokite struggled to breathe as the air drained from the ship.

"Margaret..." When he passed out from lack of air, enough oxygen returned to keep him unconscious but alive.

———

As Rivka was anger-tapping her reply, a new message came in.

Mackestray in custody. Will bring both ships to your position at the mine.

Rivka swiped her finger across her message and deleted it. She tapped different words. **Well done.**

"Shall we?" Red asked, pointing toward the rim above.

"Everything seems to be well in hand," Rivka replied. "We don't need to go down there. I'll zombie them when they bring them out."

They headed back up the hill. "Kind of anti-climactic, don't you think, Red?"

"It's a huge relief knowing those two are out of business. It's also amazing, the tons of credits crime can pay."

"Crime with a niche. Mackestray had his unique product, and no one could influence an election like him. And K'Twillis operated illegal mines. Finding exploitable resources is a difficult proposition, yet he could go right to them. In the Federation's hands, such technology could save a great deal of time over random exploration and sampling. Maybe we'll find something when we tear that freighter apart. Which reminds me, it's in Capstanian custody right now. We'll give them their exotic ore back while the Federation takes the ship."

Red and Lindy held hands as they walked. Red smiled more than usual.

"It's nice knowing that without a price on my head, random scumbags won't be taking pot shots hoping for a quick payout. I don't want to risk losing you."

"Even if I'm mean?" Lindy asked.

"Don't listen to that guy. You're mean to people who deserve it. We all are."

"He called *me* mean too," Rivka added, nodding. She stopped to glare at her security team when no one said anything. "You think he's right? You think I'm mean?" She crossed her arms and stood her ground.

"You're as mean as a fucking snake," Red blurted.

Rivka did a double-take.

"I'm Magistrate Rivka Anoa, and if you don't do what I tell you, I'll punch you in the face," Red imitated.

"I don't come across like that, do I?"

Red and Lindy chuckled together as if sharing a private joke.

Red explained, "You have to. Why can't they respect the office? Frankly, I don't know why you're not meaner. I'd start with a punch in the face and *then* make the requests."

"What he said," Lindy agreed.

"Our missions are tough," Red added.

"Cases," Rivka corrected.

"Magistrate?" Red shook a finger at her.

"I'll concede in this case alone that it was more of a mission, but we still collected evidence and built a case that I could defend before a court of law, and I will file the appropriate paperwork. When we have Mackestray in our hands, what do you want me to ask him?"

"I never thought about it," Red said. "I always expected to kill him."

"Did he intend to destroy Leed's Planet?" Lindy offered.

"I think that one may be all we need since it'll tell us what was in his mind as a civilization was brought to its knees. I want to see what Ankh has. That will put the bow on the package. I see Jhiordaan in his future."

"Not capital? He gets to live?"

"I'll judge when I see the evidence, but from what I've seen so far, his interference may have been the catalyst, but the underlying causes were there long before the Blokite appeared. He simply exploited them to his clients' advantage."

"Maybe you should be meaner?" Red suggested.

"I love the law, Vered!" The Magistrate laughed as they reached the top. She started yelling at two officers remaining with the vehicles, "You need to move all these vehicles over there."

She pointed, and they hopped. When they finished, a number of vehicles remained that would prevent *Peacekeeper's* landing.

"I have an idea." Red jogged to the haul road and climbed into the truck. It readily started. He leaned out the window. "Why didn't we move the truck and drive down instead of running along the road like idiots?"

Rivka shrugged. Red nudged the loaded truck up against the first of the vehicles and then jammed the accelerator. The car slid sideways across the lot, slamming into another vehicle and then another. Red carefully backed up and repeated the procedure until the lot was clear. He parked the truck to the side, jumping down and brushing his hands off.

The van maneuvered through the area and headed into the pit, the driver waving as he passed.

A shadow in the sky signaled the approach of the spaceships. The corvette circled before Mackestray's yacht landed near the shack, then *Peacekeeper* descended and filled the remainder of the open space. The hatch popped, and Jay ran out with Floyd bouncing after her.

"You were all magnificent!" she declared, hugging each of them. Her nose wrinkled and she pushed quickly away from Red.

He shrugged. "I know, I smell like a swamp. Tangle with an Aborginian and the stench will cling to you forever."

"I hope not forever. Not when you have a Magistrate on

your side." Lindy kissed Red's cheek. "I still love you, Stinky."

Floyd nuzzled Red's leg and then started to chew on the material. "We should have let her gnaw K'Twillis into submission."

They made their way to the ship. *Is Mackestray incapacitated?* Rivka asked.

Yes, Ankh replied. *There's enough oxygen to keep him alive, but not awake. As soon as we open the door, that will change.*

"He's out, but when the door opens, he'll get a breath of fresh air. We need to be quick about grabbing him."

"No one is quicker than me," Jay suggested.

Red handed her the zip-tie cuffs he was holding. "His arms won't fit behind his back, so cuff him in front, and I'll carry him out."

"Simple and effective," Rivka stated. "We'll be out here." *Ankh, open the hatch, please.*

The hatch popped and dropped to the ground, the inside of it acting as the stairs. Jay was gone in a flash, returning after a few seconds to usher Red inside.

"He's still out, but now he's cuffed." She bowed, and Red climbed in, making the ship look even smaller than it already was. They heard the sound of flesh striking flesh.

"Everything okay in there, Red?" Rivka shouted at the opening.

"Coming out," he replied, appearing in the hatch with his bundle of Blokite. He tossed the alien outside to land head-first on the ground. Mackestray rolled to his back and blinked at the sky. His whole focus appeared to be on his breathing.

Rivka gripped his arm to hold him down while Red and Lindy loomed over him. Floyd darted in to sniff his face.

"Did you intend to destroy Leed's Planet?"

"Destroy?" he mumbled.

Rivka struggled to parse what she was seeing in his alien mind. His intent had been to destroy reputations, throw doubt on a process so easily corruptible, and solidify his position as the one to guarantee an election victory.

"I'm sorry," she told Red. "Although people have died from his meddling, he never intended for people to die. He had already struck Leed's Planet from his resume."

"He's still scum! He put a price on my head," Red complained.

"And he'll go to Jhiordaan for the rest of his life, and that's without any of the evidence I get from Ankh."

The sergeant appeared with the first of those who had been working in the surface mine. Rivka asked one question. "What's your job?" Miners had a far different answer in their minds than those dressed in black. She tapped them quickly, one by one. "Miner, Miner, Thug, Miner..."

The thugs were pulled away and secured. The miners were corralled separately. They would have to give statements, but they also had looks of relief on their faces. Their lives had been hell working under the bat-wielding overlords. When she reached the foreman, he was the only miner who looked guilty.

She asked him a different question. "What are you hiding?"

His mind instantly shot to the bodies of those who had been killed in accidents from rushing to get the ore out that were buried in the mine.

"This one." Rivka pushed him toward an officer. "He's the foreman who allowed all this to happen. There are bodies buried down there. At least four." One of the officers grabbed him by the arm and yanked him hard enough to dislocate his shoulder. The foreman started to whimper.

They dragged him away and stuffed him into the van so they could return to the mine and he could point out where the bodies were buried.

Only one of the thugs had had enough ingenuity to lose the black and dress like a miner. He had no mental discipline, and was quickly outed and corralled with the other thugs.

"What do we do with his ship?" Red asked.

"I can confiscate it under my authority. If it was purchased using stolen funds, we'd have to find the rightful owner, but the funds weren't stolen. They were justly paid by people trying to win elections. It looks like it's the spoils of war."

"Can we have it?" Lindy asked. "You know, as a wedding present?"

Jay jumped to Lindy to wrap her in a bear hug but was unintentionally repulsed by the ever-present railgun.

"I don't see why not." Rivka smiled and waved. "Come on, then. We have places to go and people to see."

"We'll rename it, of course," Red told Lindy. "What do you think of *Anoa's Ark?*"

"I like it!"

"No," Rivka answered. "Maybe *Pampered Princess?*"

"No!" Red shot back.

"I like that one, too."

"This could take a while," Red admitted. "But look, we have a yacht!"

<u>Federation Border Station 7</u>

Rivka's datapad buzzed as her mouth hovered over a steaming concoction that she was about to eat on a dare. Her face dropped, and she set the slice back among its fellows. With a sigh, she tapped the screen.

"Nice timing," she told the familiar face. Grainger grinned back.

"It's my turn to be a bent wire inside your spacesuit!" He started to laugh, and Rivka rolled her finger to get him to hurry up. Her eyes wandered back to her lunch, and her mouth watered at the aroma that wafted to her nose. He finished with a chortle and a snort. "I wanted to compliment you on your last two cases. The information Ankh found secreted within Margaret's core guarantee that Mackestray will never again breathe free air. He is en route to Jhiordaan right now. The Federation was able to get one of their transport teams to Capstan. Sorry that took so long.

"And K'Twillis. What a nightmare! Plundering worlds for their resources! Usually, that is left to the locals or military conquerors. It chaps everyone's ass when a third-party sneaks in and does it."

"I think we burned some bridges on Capstan," Rivka replied.

"Not in the least. The Chief Constable called High Chancellor Wyatt directly with his compliments regarding your work. His hands were tied in what they could do since probable cause is one of the main tenets of their society. Combined with the licensing requirements, their people exercise more freedom than most throughout the galaxy. We could learn a thing or two from them."

"The Chief Constable?" Rivka's lips twitched into a smile. "I felt like I was railroading him."

"You received the support you needed, didn't you?"

"Since you mention it, yes. We had a van and were shuttled around. We had a tactical team when we needed it, and they stored the perps when we captured them."

"Sounds like you wanted for nothing. And now you have a yacht, too. Are you going to be like Terry Henry Walton and acquire your own fleet?"

"Terry Henry! We left him in that quagmire of Leed's Planet. I haven't called him since I left." The unspoken question hung in the air—Rivka wanted validation from Grainger that it had been okay to summon the Bad Company.

Grainger saw the meatball served up on a silver platter. He frowned and shook his head. "General Reynolds is wondering how the Magistrates are going to pay for that. Probably the price of a private yacht and a corvette. You may have to walk to your next case. Grainger out."

Rivka reached a finger toward the screen but was too slow. It turned black before she could stab Grainger's image.

"I need to make a couple of calls."

"What you need to do is eat," Doctor Toofakre told her, patiently waiting for her to finish the call. His burger sat untouched until they could eat at the same time, although his fries were half gone. She couldn't remember seeing him eat them. Rivka wondered if he had only ordered a child's portion or if he'd been adept at eating them without being seen.

She chose the latter. The dentist looked far too casual.

The Magistrate removed her slice and started to eat, barely pausing for a breath during the first slice. Then she dug into a second.

"I miss hot food when we're out there," Rivka mumbled through a mouthful of TH's Moonstokle Pie. The recipe had been picked up by most of the franchisees. "This blend of salty and sweet is to die for!"

Doctor Toofakre grimaced. "I like mine straight up. Meat and vegetables. Protein for life, food for the soul."

"Are you huffing your own nitrous again?"

"Hey!" Tyler looked around quickly to make sure no one had heard. "Don't even kid like that. I could lose my license."

"You aren't, are you?" She touched his hand. No subterfuge. The only thing he did when patients weren't there was read, but he did it kicked back in the patient's chair, reclined with his book overhead and voice-controlled. "I don't know how you stay awake reading like that!"

"Hey! Stay out of my mind." He leaned conspiratorially close. "What if you see my porn collection?"

He held out his hand and smiled evilly.

She leaned back. "You don't *have* a porn collection."

"I know. I'm boring. Startlingly dull in all ways, shapes, and forms. Maybe I can go on a case with you? You know, take a run on the wild side."

Rivka turned serious. "People die on the wild side.

Sometimes boring is the best fuel for the soul, but I'll consider taking you. The next case looks like slave trafficking. The Federation isn't real keen on slavery. We have a couple of leads that I'll be looking into when the time is right, which usually means sooner rather than later."

The End

Judge, Jury, & Executioner, Book 4
If you like this book, please leave a review. This is a new series, so the only way I can decide whether to commit more time to it is by getting feedback from you, the readers. Your opinion matters to me. Continue or not? I have only so much time to craft new stories. Help me invest that time wisely. Plus, reviews buoy my spirits and stoke the fires of creativity.

Don't stop now! Keep turning the pages as Craig talks about his thoughts on this book and the overall project called the Age of Expansion.
Your new favorite legal eagle will return!

You are still reading! Thank you so much. It doesn't get much better than that.

I think the Executioner series is my best-received series out of all that I've done. Thank you to you wonderful people for joining me. I really like this series, and enjoy writing it.

I wrote this next bit thinking about the way combat never leaves the warrior. They can go home, but they'll never leave the battlefield. Those thoughts are always hiding in the back of our minds.

Brothers in Arms

A man stands in the crisp morning. A home in the country. A breeze rustling the leaves.

"HOLD THE LINE!" echoes in the battle of his mind.

A bird lands nearby, sings, and flies to the next tree.

"Damn you! Keep firing!" Kill to live.

A hesitant sun beyond the horizon, spreading its glow.

A scream of pain. The injured cries out.

A truck negotiating a hill in the distance. Give it some gas.

"Hold pressure here. Don't give up on me."

The ground fog brightens with the first rays of dawn. No, you don't get to see the earth. Not yet.

"Help me up. I can shoot." And it is done. More rounds fired. More men cry out.

The furnace starts and runs. The cold descends to make a last stand against the day's warmth.

Day into night into day. Explosions of violence. Wince at the noise, but don't trust the silence!

Something bounds through the woods. A squirrel filling its cheeks.

The battle ends as quickly as it started. "REPORT!" For the injured. For the ammunition.

A family sleeps within. A man stands without. No sleep for him. Someone has to watch.

For the ever-present enemy. For his brothers in arms.

My sister-in-law passed away earlier today. My brother is a wreck. She had a massive stroke at sixty-five, and that was it. I fly out tomorrow to join him and hopefully help him through the initial shock. It's a challenging time, but the best thing for me is escaping into my science fiction worlds. Sometimes the real world is a bit harsh. With a good book, we can disappear for a brief time and live somewhere else, where the good guys win. I believe in karma.

And good guys who seek Justice.

Natalie Grey wants to include Bustamove in her next Barnabas story. Woohoo! You'll get a little more insight into one of the other Magistrates.

I hope everyone enjoyed this story. It was fun to write in a way that I found most relaxing. James Caplan, Micky Cocker, and Kelly O'Donnell keep me on the straight and narrow with in-process reads and ideas, language smoothing, continuity, and overall readability. They are an amazing bunch who help make me and my stories better.

No one goes on this journey alone. If it weren't for being surrounded by great people and the incredible readers who keep picking up my books, none of these stories would be possible.

Peace, fellow humans.

Please join my Newsletter (www.craigmartelle.com – please, please, please sign up!), or you can follow me on Facebook since you'll get the same opportunity to pick up the books for only 99 cents on that first day they are published.

If you liked this story, you might like some of my other books. You can join my mailing list by dropping by my website **www.craigmartelle.com** or if you have any comments, shoot me a note at craig@craigmartelle.com. I am always happy to hear from people who've read my work. I try to answer every email I receive.

If you liked the story, please write a short review for me on Amazon. I greatly appreciate any kind words, even one or two sentences go a long way. The number of reviews an ebook receives greatly improves how well an ebook does on Amazon.

Amazon – www.amazon.com/author/craigmartelle

BookBub – https://www.bookbub.com/authors/craig-martelle

Facebook – www.facebook.com/authorcraigmartelle

My web page – www.craigmartelle.com

That's it—break's over, back to writing the next book. Peace, fellow humans.

Enemy of my Enemy (co-written with Tim Marquitz) – A galactic alien military space opera (coming late summer of 2018)

Superdreadnought (co-written with Tim Marquitz) – a military space opera (coming fall of 2018)

BOOKS BY MICHAEL ANDERLE

For a complete list of books by Michael Anderle, please visit:

www.lmbpn.com/ma-books/

All LMBPN Audiobooks are Available at Audible.com and iTunes

To see all LMBPN audiobooks, including those written by Michael Anderle please visit:

www.lmbpn.com/audible